1928

. . . She slowed to a snail's pace
when she rounded the corner onto
136th Street. She was nearing the Dark Tower.
Her chest seared with pain. She limped on her
sore feet, panting. Bessie admitted to herself now
that she feared the Dark Tower more
than anything in her life. . . .

MYSTERY OF THE DARK TOWER

⚬

by
Evelyn Coleman

American Girl™

Printed in the United States of America.
00 01 02 03 04 05 RRD 10 9 8 7 6 5 4 3 2 1

History Mysteries® and American Girl™
are trademarks of Pleasant Company.

PERMISSIONS & PICTURE CREDITS
Excerpts from "The Weary Blues" appearing on pp. 42 and 51 are reprinted by
permission of Alfred A. Knopf, A Division of Random House. From *Collected Poems* by
Langston Hughes, © 1994 by the Estate of Langston Hughes.
The following individuals and organizations have generously given permission to reprint
illustrations contained in "A Peek into the Past": p. 141—*The Janitor Who Paints* (detail), National
Museum of American Art, Washington DC/Art Resource, NY; pp. 142-143—©Bettman/Corbis
(Harlem street); Corbis/Bettman-UPI (policeman); Corbis/Bettman (home); courtesy Tom Morgan,
Jazz Roots (sheet music); Schomburg Center for Research in Black Culture, The New York Public
Library (cast photo); pp. 144-145—Salamander Picture Library ("Yellow Dog Blues" cover);
©Underwood & Underwood/Corbis (Duke Ellington); courtesy Tom Morgan, Jazz Roots ("Mood
Indigo" cover); Jazz Index (Bessie Smith); The Library of Congress, #LC-USZ61-1859 DLC
(Zora Neale Hurston); *Portrait of Langston Hughes* by Winold Reiss (detail), National Portrait
Gallery, Smithsonian Institution/Art Resource, NY; pp. 146-147—*Aspects of Negro Life: An Idyll
of the Deep South* by Aaron Douglas, Art and Artifacts Division, Schomburg Center,
The New York Public Library, Astor, Lennox and Tilden Foundations; A'Lelia Bundles/
Walker Family Collection (A'Lelia Walker); Corbis (sanatorium); photograph by
Trevor Graham, University of Glasgow (Toni Morrison).

Cover and Map Illustrations: Dahl Taylor
Line Art: Greg Dearth
Editorial Direction: Yvette La Pierre and Peg Ross
Art Direction: Jane Varda
Design: Jane Varda and Lynne Wells

Library of Congress Cataloging-in-Publication Data

Coleman, Evelyn, 1948-
Mystery of the Dark Tower / by Evelyn Coleman.
p. cm. — (History mysteries ; 6)
"American girl."
Summary: In 1928, when her father tears her and her brother from their mother in
North Carolina and takes them to live with aunts in Harlem, twelve-year-old Bessie is
trapped in a strange place, especially after her father mysteriously disappears.

ISBN 1-58485-085-X (hc) — ISBN 1-58485-084-1 (pbk.)
[1. Harlem (New York, N.Y.)—Fiction. 2. Parent and child—Fiction. 3. Afro-Americans—
Fiction. 4. Harlem Renaissance—Fiction. 5. Mystery and detective stories.]
I. Title. II. Series.
PZ7.C6746 My 2000 [Fic]—dc21 99-055810

To the six siblings of my mother, Annie S. Coleman,
who all died of tuberculosis in the days when
it was considered a shameful disease

And to Bessie Carol Coble Scott, a high school
classmate of mine, who despite an illness in our senior year
still graduated with honors. Bessie, you were one of
the bravest people I knew in high school!

TABLE OF CONTENTS

BESSIE'S WORLD
Harlem in 1928

Rent party

Uptown Harlem

Bessie's neighborhood

CHAPTER **I**

MISERY

Bessie Carol Coulter tossed and turned in the wrought iron bed she shared with her younger brother, Eddie. The smell of honeysuckle wafted in through the open window on a cool spring breeze. Bessie sat up and peered out the window. The full moon and stars lit up the night sky above the tobacco fields. She fell back on her pillow and pulled the patchwork quilt up over her head.

Then Bessie lowered the quilt slowly and peeped upward, toward the ceiling. She always did this before she fell asleep on the nights the full moon allowed her to see. And each time, even though she knew what was up there, she felt a giggle of surprise.

The ceiling was indigo blue with tiny gold stars all over it. Papa had painted it for her last birthday when she turned twelve. A horse with a long flowing mane galloped across the ceiling. A picket fence covered with wisteria, her favorite flower, bordered one edge. On one side Papa had painted a bright yellow half-moon.

When Papa showed it to Bessie and Eddie, he said he wanted his children to sleep under beauty every night. Papa was always saying things like that. And even though the room wasn't fancy and there wasn't anything but one rickety bed and an old dresser in it, the ceiling made Bessie's room the most beautiful room in the world.

Bessie concentrated on the ceiling and wished she couldn't hear the rumbling thunder coming from her parents' bedroom. Her grandma always used to say, "If they's be thunder, lightning done already come." It was times like this when Bessie missed Grandma the most. Since Grandma's death last year, Bessie felt more and more stabs of loneliness in her heart, because there was no one to talk with anymore. Even though Bessie felt close to her mama and papa, Grandma was the only one who believed children should be seen *and* heard. Bessie hated being treated like a child who had no sense.

Bessie couldn't stand the angry sounds from the other room anymore. She squeezed her eyes shut and put her hands over her ears. *Maybe parents are the ones who shouldn't be heard,* Bessie thought. She tried to hear her grandma's voice talking softly to her and Eddie, instead of the stormy argument of her parents.

"Bessie Carol and Eddie," Grandma would say, sitting on the edge of the bed while tucking the quilt up under their chins, "this here quilt is made from clothes your papa and his sisters wore when they was no bigger'n you two. As long as you with your family, everything is always gonna be all right."

Bessie had always believed everything Grandma told her. But now she wasn't so sure. Bessie's parents had been arguing for weeks. Bessie knew her mama, Martha Coulter, was unhappy. And so was her papa, Edward Coulter Senior. What she didn't know was why.

This week had been the worst. Mama had been cooped up in her bedroom. Papa said Mama was sick with a terrible cold and needed her rest. Neither Bessie nor Eddie had been allowed to see her. They weren't even allowed to talk to her through the door. Papa was the only one who went in and out of the room. But Bessie never heard tell of nobody not being able to see their children just because of a cold. Something was wrong. Bessie could feel it. Bessie decided that tomorrow morning she would ask Mama what was the matter, even if she had to ask through the door.

Bessie was truly worried, especially since their neighbor Mrs. Cannon went away and left her husband and children two weeks ago. Everybody in church said that Mrs. Cannon wasn't coming back, but nobody said why. But Bessie wasn't dumb. She'd overheard the older people at church talking about families breaking up. "Separating," they called it.

Bessie paid attention to what grown folks said. She

heard them whispering more and more about the year 1928, like it was mean and nasty. They talked about how the times were bringing mighty changes to the South. They said the government was taking back the few rights the colored folks had, so folks were running from the South by the truckloads. Men and women were all going north to find work and make better lives for themselves.

Sometimes they'd take their families, but oftentimes the husband or the wife went alone. A few people had been gossiping, or "syndicating," that Mr. and Mrs. Cannon had separated and that Mrs. Cannon went north, leaving Mr. Cannon to take care of the three younguns by himself.

The loud crash of the front door slamming startled Bessie out of her thinking. Eddie was only seven and such a sound sleeper, he didn't even stir. Had Papa left? Was he *that* mad with Mama? Bessie could hear Mama coughing in her room. She could hear Papa stomping onto the porch.

Then Bessie recognized another voice outside. It was Mr. Cannon.

She threw the covers back and got up on her knees so she could peer out the window. The thin feather-bed mattress didn't give much under her bony knees. Bessie couldn't see anything. She hoisted the window up higher and climbed out. She knew how to do it quietly. She'd done it many times before when she wanted to sneak out to the barn to sleep with her horse, Brownie. She had to be real quiet so as not to wake the chickens. Bessie knew that if she woke them, they'd make so much fuss that Papa would come around the house to see why they were squawking.

Bessie's bare feet stung as she hit the ground. She bent down low and crept quietly toward the front of the wood-framed house. The barn and chicken coop were only a few clotheslines away from the house. When Bessie neared the porch, she heard Mr. Cannon talking.

"I know you ain't wanting to do it. But I'm telling you, it's the best for your chillun, son. You don't want your chillun to be here." Mr. Cannon stopped and spit a plug of tobacco onto the bare dirt yard before he spoke again.

"I knows how you feel. But it ain't nothing else to do. Your time's done run out. She ain't gonna be able to go off and leave you like my Sally done. You gonna have to leave her."

"I can't do it," Papa said. But it didn't sound like Papa. He was talking funny, like his voice was cracking open with each word. "Martha wants me to leave, too, but man, I can't. I tell you, I just can't."

Bessie's hands flew up to her face to hold back the yelp that sprang from her mouth. She stood still, not breathing, as she heard Papa ask, "What was that?"

"Just a dog yelping," Mr. Cannon replied.

"I reckon," said Papa, looking toward the side of the house where Bessie crouched.

Bessie moved closer to the shadows of the house. The

yard's dirt was packed hard and felt cool and slick under her feet from the early evening dew.

Mr. Cannon began speaking again. "Now you go on and tell Martha you leaving her, Big Ed," he said, slapping Papa on the back with a thud of his heavy hand. "Everything will be all right. You'll see. Time's a-wasting."

Why was he talking Papa into leaving their mama? Maybe it was because *his* wife left *him,* Bessie thought. But Bessie didn't want Papa to leave Mama. Bessie sure wasn't leaving Mama. She didn't care what anyone said, Bessie Carol Coulter would not go anywhere, not without her mama.

Bessie needed to do something. She picked up a rock. She wanted to hurl it at Mr. Cannon's fat head. He was a big man, almost as tall as Papa. A little rock wouldn't really do much damage to him, just make him shut up his old turkey mouth.

Bessie fingered the rock. She burned to let it fly. Bessie was known for throwing rocks dead on target. She turned around and threw the rock as hard as she could toward the apple tree. She wanted to knock the tree's bark off. But when she heard the *ping* of the rock, it didn't make her feel better.

Bessie sat down on the dirt, wishing Grandma were still with them. Grandma wouldn't let Papa leave Mama.

Bessie's old hurt rose up like a water moccasin out of the fishing pond. She thought about the day of

Grandma's funeral. Bessie could see her grandma's coffin sitting in the front room, draped with one of her favorite lace tablecloths, a bunch of white roses on top. That day Bessie's mama came out and sat with her under the big old willow.

"You mad?" she asked Bessie.

Bessie nodded her head yes.

"She wasn't my blood mama," Bessie's mama said, "but since Memaw died she's been the only mama I knew. I think I'm mad, too. So what you want to do about it?"

Bessie shrugged her shoulders.

"Well, you know what your grandma would say. She'd say, 'You ain't really mad. You sad.' We both just sad."

Bessie shrugged again. Then she looked directly into Mama's eyes and said, "*I'm* really mad."

"Me too, then," Mama said, standing up. She picked up a rock. Mama leaned back and threw the rock hard at the side of the barn. *Boom,* it thundered. "Your turn," Mama said.

Bessie chose a rock off the ground, leaned back, and fired it. *Bam.* The barn door shuddered. The two of them threw rocks until they both were too tired to lift their arms. Then they slumped down beside the willow's trunk and cried while holding on to each other. That was the closest Bessie had ever felt to Mama.

And now Papa was talking about leaving Mama. Bessie couldn't think of nothing to do to fix this. Then it was like

hear Grandma's voice, saying "If anger come
you so hard you can't think, then there ain't
but one thing left to do. Let it go. Cry it on out." Bessie
whimpered into her hands. She cried for Grandma, Eddie,
Mama, Papa, and herself.

Bessie finally wiped her face with the tail of her
pajama top and sneaked back into her room. She got in
bed and curled up around Eddie so they made an S shape
together. She put her arms around her little brother and
held back her sobs. At long last, she fell asleep.

⟅⟆

Bessie woke in a haze of someone shaking her.

"Bessie. Bessie, get up now, girl. Come on."

It was Papa.

Bessie squeezed her eyes tighter. Maybe he would
leave her be.

Papa lit the bedside lamp. "Bessie, I need you to get
up and get ready. Then get your brother ready. We got to
go. Hurry up now."

Bessie stretched her eyes as wide as sleep would let
her. "What do you mean, Papa? Where we going?"

"We're going on the train. We ain't got much time.
Come on, baby girl."

This was serious. Papa only used "baby girl" when he
didn't want to say what he had to say.

"Papa, what about Mama?" Bessie asked as Mr. Cannon's words popped into her head. "Is Mama going on the train, too?"

Papa's eyes filled with tears. "Baby girl, I ain't got time to talk now. We got to leave. The train, it don't wait for folks. Come on now."

Papa yanked the quilt off the bed and bundled it under his arm. He began stuffing things into an old suitcase. He closed the worn suitcase and walked to the door with it.

"Mama's gotta pick out Eddie's clothes to wear," Bessie said, tears coming to her eyes.

Papa said softly, "Your mama can't come right now, so you pick them out for Eddie. Now hurry up."

Bessie stood very still. "I ain't leaving Mama, Papa. I just ain't," she said, her voice barely above a whisper.

Papa turned around. With quick, long steps he walked back to the bed. "Bessie Carol Coulter," he said, raising his voice, "you gonna do what I tell you. I said get dressed and help your brother. You both better be ready by the time I'm back."

Bessie cried as she pulled on her clothes. She sniffled loudly as she helped Eddie get dressed. Eddie sniffled along with his sister. Bessie put on her socks and shoes and hurriedly pulled on her jacket. All the while she was thinking, *Papa can't leave Mama. They's married. Mama always say, "Papa the best man in the whole world."*

"What's h-h-happening, Bessie?" Eddie asked.

"Don't worry. I'll be with you." Bessie clasped Eddie's hand and squeezed until the blood drained from their fingers.

Papa rushed back into the room. "Come on. Hurry. Mr. Cannon's taking us to the train in his truck." He grabbed Eddie up.

"But Papa," Bessie cried, "where's Mama? Ain't we gonna even say good-bye?"

Papa didn't look down at her. He took her hand and pulled her by the arm through the house, toward the grumbling truck outside. Bessie whipped her head around, looking for Mama.

"Mama?" Bessie called, trying to pull her hand out of Papa's grip. "Mama!" she yelled, louder.

Eddie struggled. "M-m-mama!" he called, tears streaming down his face.

Bessie jerked away from Papa and raced to the bedroom door. She yanked the door latch. It was bolted. She thought she heard a sob from behind the door. "Maaamaa," Bessie cried again, frantic now. "Mama, come on out, please," Bessie pleaded, wildly pulling on the door. "Mama, come on!"

"Here now, child," Mr. Cannon said, snatching Bessie up by the waist. "Your mama gonna be all right. Come on now."

Bessie barely heard him. "Maaamaa. Maaamaa. Come with us, Mama," she called, struggling to free herself from Mr. Cannon's clawish hands. Bessie felt as though her heart were breaking into tiny little pieces, like nuts cracked open at Christmastime. "Maaamaa. Maaamaa," she screamed as Mr. Cannon dragged her out onto the porch.

Eddie banged his fists into Papa's chest, trying to get down. Mr. Cannon plopped Bessie onto the truck seat. He jumped in and revved the engine. Papa, still holding Eddie tightly, leaped in on the passenger side. Bessie could see her brother's face turning red as he yelled. Bessie screamed and yelled with him.

As the truck lurched forward, Bessie spotted Brownie at the edge of the fence. The mare kicked up dust and whinnied as if she knew what was happening. Bessie felt as confused as a bumblebee trapped inside a jar. She squirmed to look back out the truck window as they rumbled up the dirt road. The truck took them past their cornfields and the rows of string beans and watermelons. They rode out past the pig trough and the field where their two milk cows grazed and along the edge of the pond toward town.

Bessie was afraid she might be smelling the sweetness of the apple orchards and the honeysuckle for the last time. She cried as she listened to the distant call of a whippoor-will singing them a good-bye song. Finally, exhausted, she cried herself to sleep.

When Bessie woke up, they were in town. She peered out the truck window and saw the man who sat high up in the little wooden house beside the railroad tracks. His job was to put the wooden arm down or up, to let people know if it was safe to cross the train tracks. Bessie usually loved seeing the man in his little house and always waved to him. But not tonight. *I wish the man would make the train stay right here and never leave Burlington, North Carolina,* she thought as Papa lifted her up on one hip and Eddie on the other and carried them crying into the colored section of the ugly iron train.

Bessie wiped her tears with her sleeve as she heard the rumbling of the train on the tracks and the whistle blowing. The bouncing vibration of the train's wheels reminded Bessie of riding Brownie. She wondered if Brownie had knocked down the fence to follow her. But Bessie knew she hadn't. Papa built sturdy fences.

Bessie finally sat up straight and looked around the car. A few people were eating from shoeboxes as though they were having a picnic. Some people were asleep, and others read from Bibles.

"Where we going, Papa?" Bessie asked weakly, choking back tears. But even as she asked the question, she knew. This had to be the Southern Crescent. It came through Burlington in the wee hours of the morning, five days a week. The whistle always *whoooo*ed when it got into town. After picking up a few passengers, it pulled out, singing its whistling song.

This was the train Mama told her about, the one that connected the South to the North. Bessie had never been on a train before. She'd always dreamed of riding on the mighty Southern Crescent, but not like this—not without Mama.

Papa whispered to her, "Bessie Carol, I promise everything will be all right." He added weakly, "It'll be fine. Honest."

Bessie laid her head back in the crook of Papa's arm. Papa rubbed her head gently, the way he did when she fell asleep on him at church while the choir sang the words of her favorite song, "Amazing Grace."

Bessie raised her head just a little, enough to see where Eddie was. He lay sleeping on the seat next to them, leaning against Papa.

"But what about Mama? Where's Mama?" Bessie whispered.

"Your mama's home," Papa said. "Your mama can't come just yet. But she gonna come. Soon."

"Why didn't she say good-bye?"

"Mama needs to stay in her room and rest," Papa said.

"Where we going? Where we going without Mama?"

Papa turned his head toward the window. For a minute he sounded like he was choking. Then, still gazing out the window, he said, "We're going to Harlem. Harlem, New York. We're staying with your Aunt Esther and Aunt Nellie for a spell. Aunt Esther won't be there when we get there. She's in Boston seeing about her daughter. Aunt Nellie is expecting us, though."

"I don't want to go to Harlem, Papa," Bessie said. "I don't want to be in New York."

Papa hugged Bessie close. "You gonna love New York. You'll see. It'll be all right. I promise."

Bessie laid her head down on Papa's knee. She gently touched Eddie's hand and laced her fingers in his. Eddie slept on, but Bessie knew he felt her. It was their sign that no matter what happened, they would stand together.

There was no way to make going to Harlem be all right, no matter how many promises Papa made. Bessie was not even impressed when they changed trains in Washington, D.C., to the Pennsylvania Railroad. It didn't matter to her that now they could sit in any car, not just the one for coloreds. The truth was, Bessie hated Harlem already. Nothing could ever be all right again—not without Mama—and never, ever in old, stinking, ratty Harlem.

CHAPTER 2

HATING HARLEM

From the moment Bessie stepped off the train in New York's Grand Central Station, she struggled to remember how angry she was about coming to Harlem and to feel the pain of missing Mama. But she had to admit, she'd only seen one other thing in her life that made her so excited—a kaleidoscope in the general feed store back home in Burlington. When she'd picked up the long cylinder and placed her eye where the man showed her, her heart had burst open with joy—so many colors, so many shapes, so wonderful! That's what Bessie saw when she first laid eyes on New York City.

Papa hustled them out to the street. He put his fingers into his mouth and gave a shrill whistle. A colored man driving a car swerved over to the side of the street and hopped out.

"Good afternoon, sir," he said. He helped Papa put

the bags in the trunk, and directed them into the backseat.

"Who is he, Papa?" Bessie asked.

"He works driving people in this taxi," Papa said, holding Bessie and Eddie close to him.

As they drove, the taxi driver pointed out statues and buildings. Bessie stared out the window in amazement. Iron posts with white bulbs attached to them stood along streets that were paved. The streets even had places for people to walk. Papa said they were called sidewalks. People rushed along the sidewalks, going in all directions. Cars bunched together like metal cows, honking their horns instead of mooing. The buildings were all brick. Some were so tall they looked as if they were pushing up into the clouds. It sure wasn't like the dirt streets of Burlington, where Bessie had lived all her life.

After riding for a while, the driver announced proudly, "This is the famous Lenox Avenue in Harlem."

Bessie was surprised to see a colored police officer directing traffic in the middle of the street. He looked important in his crisp uniform with shiny buttons. And he was telling the white drivers which way to go, too!

Bessie's grandma used to say, "Ain't nothing worse than wanting to be mad and feeling glad instead." That's just how Bessie felt when she, Eddie, and Papa pulled up in front of the stone house at 124th Street in Harlem. Bessie had never imagined that her aunts lived in such a fine house. Green ivy climbed the tall building, like wisteria vines on an arbor, and other houses crowded it on both sides. Steps led to two doors, and over the doors were pale stone arches that looked like crowns.

When Papa knocked on one of the doors, a woman not much taller than Bessie appeared. Her hair was completely straight and hung down past her ears.

"Lord," she said, grinning. "Come on in. If you ain't a sight for sore eyes!" she continued loudly. "This must be Bessie, and this is little Eddie. Why, I ain't seen you children in a month of Sundays. Get on in here and give your Aunt Nellie a hug."

Bessie and Eddie hugged their papa's sister.

"Go on," Aunt Nellie said. "Look around at your new house while I talk to your papa for a spell."

Bessie and Eddie held hands, their fingers laced together.

"Go on. Have a look around," Papa said.

Her aunts' house had four spacious rooms with mantled fireplaces, plus a kitchen. The walls were covered with what appeared to be flowered satin. When Eddie and Bessie finished looking at the pretty rooms, they stopped short near a set of stairs that led up. They could hear their aunt whispering. But even her whispers were loud.

"You right, Big Ed," Aunt Nellie was saying. "It's a shame about your wife. A real shame."

Bessie held her finger up to her lips, so Eddie
would know not to make a sound. She motioned with
her hand for him to stay put. Bessie tiptoed toward the
room where Papa and Aunt Nellie were talking.

Aunt Nellie said, "Lord, you got to be glad there's a
roof over her head. But ain't nothing you can do. You
had to leave your wife, Ed. And now, you've got to think
about the children."

Papa broke into tears. Aunt Nellie hugged him.

Bessie had never seen her papa cry. This was even worse
than she had thought. Were her parents truly separated?
Is that why Mama wouldn't say good-bye?

Bessie looked back at Eddie. He was hopping from one
foot to the other. Then he lost his balance and crashed
into a tall vase on the floor by the stairs. The sound brought
Papa and Aunt Nellie running.

"I-I-I've got to g-g-go," Eddie said, flashing an apolo-
getic look toward Bessie.

Bessie knew Eddie felt bad about being clumsy. A few
people back home thought Eddie was dumb. Bessie hated
for them to say that about her brother. He might be slow
to talk, but he wasn't nowhere near being dumb. He just
didn't like talking to strangers because it took him so long
to get his words out. If he was sad, mad, or nervous, he
stuttered even more.

"Son, look what you done," Papa said, staring at the
broken pieces of the fancy vase.

"Oh, my," said Aunt Nellie. "Esther is going to kill us all."

"I'll handle her," Papa said. "Don't worry."

"Come on, follow me," Aunt Nellie said, walking up the stairs. "I'll show you where he can go."

Papa grabbed Eddie's hand and followed Aunt Nellie up the staircase. Bessie followed behind them. She pulled on Papa's sleeve. "Papa," Bessie whispered, "Aunt Nellie doesn't know he means he has to pee."

"She knows what he means, Bessie," Papa said, turning to smile at her. "They have an inside toilet upstairs."

"Oh," Bessie said, trying to sound like she didn't care. But she did. She'd never been in a house that had an upstairs. And she'd never been to an outhouse that was inside!

Aunt Nellie led Papa and Eddie into a room. She walked back out alone, leaving Eddie and Papa inside the bathroom.

"You sure is a pretty girl. You look just like your . . ." Aunt Nellie paused. "I bet y'all hungry," she finished quickly.

A loud whooshing sound erupted from the bathroom. Bessie jumped.

"Don't worry, that's just the toilet flushing," Aunt Nellie said.

When the door opened, Papa said, "I'm going down and clean that mess up."

"I'll get the children washed up for supper," Aunt Nellie said. Then she took Bessie into the bathroom with Eddie.

Bessie was speechless. The room didn't look like any outhouse she'd ever seen. There were no spiders or snakes. And there was even a pot of flowers. Bessie couldn't believe that water came all the way upstairs and out the two spigots. One was for cold water and the other was for hot. Back home they had to bring water in from the well and heat it on the woodstove.

"This is bath salt for you and Eddie to use later," Aunt Nellie said, scooping a few capfuls to show them. "It'll help you relax and sleep like you were babies. Lord, what am I saying—you are babies."

"No, we're not," Bessie said. "We're big children. I'm almost grown, Aunt Nellie. I'll be thirteen on my birthday. Papa said you got married when you was thirteen."

Aunt Nellie turned around slowly. "You're right. Of course you aren't babies. But don't let your papa hear you saying that," she said, smiling. She leaned down closer to them. "That'll be our little secret."

After supper, Bessie took a bath and got ready for bed. By the time her head hit the pillow, she could barely keep her eyes open. Papa came into the room quietly to say good night.

"You and your brother asleep?"

"No, sir," Bessie said.

Eddie shook his head.

"I got something for you two." He handed them each a little handmade wooden frame.

Bessie's eyes filled with tears as she studied her frame. "Papa, did you draw this picture of me and Mama?" Bessie asked, almost whispering.

"Yes," Papa said softly. "And I drew one of Eddie with Mama too, so's you both could have a piece of Mama with you."

"It's beautiful, Papa," Bessie said.

"Th-thank you, Papa," Eddie said and hugged the picture to his chest.

"Papa, why didn't Mama come with us?" Bessie asked.

"You can't be worried about that. Children don't need to know grown folks' business. Your mama wouldn't like that. She'd just want you to be a good girl. Now stop asking questions. I'm going out early in the morning to look for work, so I won't see you tomorrow until late. But Aunt Nellie will take care of you."

Bessie thought she saw tears in Papa's eyes. "Papa, you all right?"

"Don't worry about me. And you two gonna be all right, too. Look what else I brought for you," Papa said, unfolding Grandma's quilt. He spread it over them before kissing them good night.

After Papa left, Bessie lay very still until the only thing

she could hear was the creaking of the house's bones and Eddie's soft snoring. It was hot under the quilt, but Bessie didn't care. She closed her eyes and drifted off to sleep, holding her picture of Mama and hearing Grandma saying, "As long as you with your family, everything is gonna be all right." This time Bessie didn't believe a word of it.

The next few days were like a dream, except Bessie was awake.

Aunt Nellie rustled them up bright and early each morning. The first morning, Aunt Nellie showed them the rest of the house. She even showed them her bedroom and her dresser with her makeup, perfumes, fancy notepaper, and pen on it.

At breakfast she always chattered on about this and that. Right after breakfast she would say, "Hurry. Get dressed now. Let's go air out. Once your Aunt Esther gets back, there won't be a lot of airing out. Your aunt, she don't cotton to but two things—housework and church."

At first, Bessie didn't feel like airing out. But soon the exciting sights, sounds, and smells of Harlem made her forget her troubles for a while.

Lenox Avenue was always packed with people airing out. Bessie loved seeing the peanut man, who walked down the street pushing a black baby carriage for a cart.

She smiled when she heard him call out, "Peanuts! Peanuts! Get your hot peanuts!" And then there was the crab man, dressed in a white apron and carrying a basket that was filled with hot fried crabs and covered with a white towel.

Aunt Nellie took them for rides on a train called a subway that went under the ground. One day they rode the trolley, which was like a train on tracks except it wiggled down the center of the street.

The storefronts had wide glass windows with signs plastered on them. A man sat on the corner with a wooden box propped up and shined people's shoes for three cents. Bessie couldn't help looking down at her dusty brown oxfords as they passed.

Bessie and Eddie stared and giggled with each other at almost everything. But sometimes Bessie would see a woman who reminded her of Mama. Bessie's hand would automatically finger the necklace Mama had given her, and she'd go back to wondering about why Mama hadn't come.

She'd recall Papa's words to Mr. Cannon that Mama wanted him to leave. Why? Why would Mama want Papa to leave and bring them with him? And why didn't she say good-bye? It didn't make sense. Bessie thought about the night, a few weeks before they left for Harlem, when she'd felt Mama slip something over her head while Bessie was supposed to be sleeping. After she heard Mama tiptoe out, Bessie sat up in bed and felt around her neck. Mama had put her Memaw necklace, a dime with a hole in it, strung on a cord, around Bessie's neck.

This wasn't just any old necklace. Memaw, Mama's mama, had put this dime necklace around Mama's neck when Mama was ten years old. She had told Bessie that she'd never taken it off since the day Memaw gave it to her.

The next day Bessie had asked Mama, "Why did you give me your Memaw necklace?"

"It's time you was wearing it," Mama answered. "Now don't be asking me no questions. I'm the mama here. And when I say it's time, it's time."

Maybe Mama knew Papa was leaving soon and taking them with him. Maybe it was Mama's way of saying good-bye. The thought made Bessie shiver.

As their first month in Harlem passed, Bessie, Eddie, and Aunt Nellie settled into a routine. Papa was gone most of the time, out looking for work. Bessie and Eddie liked to sit outside on the stoop in the summer sun. They enjoyed watching the people walk by. One day an old man with gray hair walked past. He was strutting with his head held high, wearing a nice brown suit and white shirt. He tipped his skinny-brimmed hat to them as he passed.

"Howdy, sir," Bessie and Eddie said. They watched him

continue down the street and go into the house on the corner.

Just then, a group of children came running up the street and stopped in front of the stoop. A tall boy held a key over his head. A plump girl jumped up and down, trying to grab the key while the other children laughed.

Bessie could see the girl was about to cry. The look on her face reminded Bessie of Eddie when children teased him about his stuttering.

Bessie stood up. "Give her the key."

"Stay out of this," the tall boy said. "It ain't your business."

"I'm making it my business," Bessie said. "Now give her the key or I'll—"

"Or you'll what?" a girl said.

"Or I'll—" Bessie picked up a chunk of brick. "See that sign over yonder?" she asked. "If I can hit the center of the sign, then you give her back her key."

"You can't even hit near the sign," one girl scoffed.

"She can't hit it. She's just a girl," a boy said.

"A skinny girl, too," another boy added.

"Yeah. Go ahead," the tall boy said, grinning. "If you even get close, we'll go."

Bessie leaned back, sured-up her footing, and let the fragment of brick fly.

The board shook. A dent appeared dead in the center.

The children looked from one to another and took

off running. The tall boy threw the key back. He stopped running just long enough to see Bessie snatch the key out of the air.

Bessie offered the plump girl the key. She was sitting on the steps next to Eddie now, sniffling. The girl's hair, which she wore in two braids, was long and silky, but it was her skin that caught Bessie's attention. It was dark like Bessie's, but it looked smooth as a piece of glass.

"Thank you. I appreciate your kindness," the girl said, wiping her eyes. The girl's talking sounded like she was singing a song.

"Where you from?" Bessie asked.

"I'm from here now. I live in this building. My parents brought me here three years ago, when I was eleven. We are from the British West Indies. We have just returned from our vacation there this week."

"What's your name?"

"Lillian Moore," the girl said, brightening. She reached out her hand.

Bessie shook it.

"Why were those children bothering you?" Bessie asked, sitting back down on the steps.

"Because they are ignorant. Just because I am from some place other than America, they pick on me."

"I-I-I-I know what th-th-that f-feels like," Eddie said.

Lillian looked confused. "Why is he talking like that?"

"He's trying to tell you he's different, too," Bessie said.

"He stutters, and people sometimes tease him about it."

"Then he's right. We are alike," Lillian said.

Eddie smiled.

Pointing to Aunt Nellie's door, Lillian asked, "Do you live next door now?"

"I don't really know," Bessie said. She felt dumb for not knowing how to answer. And sad that she even had to think about it.

Suddenly Lillian's eyes widened and her mouth dropped open. "Look," she said, pointing up the street. "Here she comes."

"Here *who* comes?" Bessie asked, following Lillian's gaze to a woman walking in their direction. The woman was tall and slender with long, long black hair. Her complexion was like the dark bark of a tree. Her dress had red, yellow, and green birds flying all over it. Her body swayed as she walked toward them. She was very pretty.

"No!" Lillian whispered through clenched teeth. "Don't let her see you looking. Are you crazy?"

"Why c-c-can't we l-look at her?" Eddie asked.

"Quick. Lower your head," Lillian whispered as the woman neared them. "Don't look in her face. She's a hoodoo woman from the Caribbean islands. She could turn us into frogs or something."

Bessie remembered Grandma talking about hoodoo women back home. They used roots and herbs to put spells, or conjures, on people.

"Sometimes Miss Flo does things to people," Lillian continued.

"Things like what?" Bessie asked, almost not wanting to know.

Lillian shrugged. "*Things.* I've heard my mother talking about it. She says Miss Flo can make a man fall in love with a woman he doesn't even like. Or make a man sick, like he has a stomach full of snakes, if he's done something bad. Or, if a woman wants to make a man do a certain thing, Miss Flo can put a root on him and make him do whatever that woman wants."

Miss Flo kept walking toward them. Then she stopped in front of the steps. Bessie, Eddie, and Lillian held their breath.

"Good morning," Miss Flo said in a voice as pretty as Lillian's.

Bessie felt torn up inside. Back home, she was taught it was disrespectful not to look at your elders' faces when they were talking to you. And if you disrespected them, not only would they whip you, but your parents would too, when they found out about it. Being turned into a frog might feel better than getting two whippings. Trembling, Bessie looked up. "Good morning, ma'am."

"You Nellie's niece and nephew. You two beautiful children. Please, tell your auntie me see her later," the woman said.

"Yes, ma'am," Bessie said.

The woman smiled slightly and nodded. "I sure Miss Lillian here told you all about me."

"Yes, ma'am, she did," Bessie said. "I mean, no, ma'am."

"Yeah, me see," the woman said, directing her gaze toward Lillian. "Well, I best run along. I got me a leg to fix."

Bessie, Eddie, and Lillian watched her walk to the house on the corner where the gray-haired man had gone. They stared until they saw her go inside. Then they all let out a sigh of relief.

"What k-k-kind of leg is she talking about f-f-fixing?" Eddie asked.

"She might be talking about *your* leg," Bessie teased.

"Shhh. You must not tease about that," Lillian said. "She might hear you."

"How?" Bessie said. "She's all the way inside her house."

"I told you," Lillian said. "She has great hoodoo power."

"I didn't mean to let Miss Flo know you'd been talking about her," Bessie said. "I'm sorry."

"We will all be sorry if we are *ribbit*ing tonight," Lillian said.

Suddenly a deep croaking sound came out of Eddie's mouth. It sounded just like a bullfrog in the spring.

Lillian gasped. "He sounds just like a real frog."

"Eddie's good at imitating," Bessie said.

Just then, the gray-haired man came out of Miss Flo's house and down her steps. Bessie and Eddie stared, speechless, as the man walked past them. He hobbled along, supported by a crutch. He slowly made his way up the street.

"What in the world is the matter with you two?" Lillian asked. "You look like you've seen a ghost."

Bessie could not find her voice. Keeping her hand low, she pointed at the man.

"What?" Lillian said. "You've never seen a man like that before?"

"B-b-but h-h-h-h-he . . ." Eddie began.

"Hurry, what are you saying?" Lillian said.

Bessie finally whispered, "That man had two legs when he went inside Miss Flo's house. And now—he only has one!"

They all three gawked. His right pant leg was tied neatly in a knot at the knee. Bessie shivered. Eddie grimaced. And Lillian looked like her eyes would pop out. She made a cross over her heart with her right hand.

"I told you," she whispered.

Bessie wanted to get inside, away from the scary woman who put spells on people. "I hear Aunt Nellie calling us," she fibbed.

"I didn't hear anything," Lillian said.

"I-I-I did," Eddie said, pulling Bessie by the hand into the house. "C-c-come on, Bessie."

Inside the door, Bessie squeezed Eddie's fingers. "Thanks," she whispered, just as she heard Aunt Nellie calling them for real.

CHAPTER 3

SOUNDS IN THE NIGHT

That night Bessie dreamed of hoodoo women and one-legged men. She awoke from the fitful dream, startled by an unfamiliar sound. Bessie heard the sound again. Was someone downstairs?

She shook Eddie. "Come on. I heard something."

Eddie frowned and turned over, pulling the covers up over his head. It was no use. When Eddie was asleep, he was hard to wake up.

Bessie pulled on the robe Aunt Nellie had given her and tiptoed slowly downstairs. She listened, but she didn't hear the sound again. The heavy drapes pulled shut made it difficult to see. Bessie felt her way by touching the wall. She didn't want to bump into anything and wake Aunt Nellie or Papa.

Bessie moved to the parlor window and parted the drapes to peer out. Outside, a few feet away, was Papa.

He was leaning on a shiny black car, talking to a tall woman in a fancy dress with a fur slung around her shoulders—and it wasn't Mama. Papa stopped for a moment, having a coughing spell, and turned toward the window.

Bessie slid back and quickly pulled the drapes shut. Then, peeping through them, Bessie watched the woman patting Papa on his back. When he finally stopped coughing, the woman hugged him.

A hot burning flame jumped into Bessie's stomach. Why was this woman hugging Papa? No one should hug Papa but his family. Then Papa hugged the woman again.

Bessie felt lower than a scolded dog. She couldn't tell Eddie about this. Not only were Mama and Papa separated, but now Papa was seeing another woman. Why else would Papa hug this woman who wasn't his relative?

Bessie wished she hadn't come downstairs. This room used to be her favorite room in the house. But she would never feel the same about it again. Bessie slid down beside the window. She pulled her knees into her chest. Bessie could see the pretty rose satin settee in front of the fireplace, but she hated it now. The heart-shaped white lace pinned on the arms of all the chairs looked silly, the fancy carved tables ugly. The curtains on the windows and the flowered rugs looked heavy and suffocating. Bessie would rather be back home, where all the

furniture was hewed from plain old wood, and the curtains
sewn from muslin by Mama.

Bessie could see Mama in her mind. Had Papa forgotten
Mama already? What was happening to Mama and Papa?
Back home, they used to be so happy. Every night at supper,
Papa would say something like, "I bet y'all children don't
even know you got the most beautiful flower in the world
sitting right here at the table with you."

Bessie and Eddie would just smile, because they knew
what Papa was going to say next.

"Your mama. She make a rose look like a wilting weed
on a hot summer night." Then Mama would giggle just like
a little girl.

But in the weeks before they left for Harlem, Papa
would eat the entire meal without saying one of his
"sugar-sweets." In fact, he would hardly say a word at
supper. Yes, Bessie could see it now. Things between
Mama and Papa had changed even before Papa brought
them to Harlem. Bessie twisted her hair while thinking.
Aunt Nellie never mentioned Mama coming to Harlem.
And now Papa never said it anymore. Bessie was beginning to think Mama wasn't coming to Harlem.

Bessie decided not to tell Eddie what she had seen
tonight. No, there was no need to put that picture in
Eddie's head, like it sat in hers. Maybe her parents were
right. Maybe children shouldn't be in grown folks' business,
because it sure did hurt.

❧

The next day Bessie moped around, keeping her secret to herself. After they'd eaten supper, Bessie and Eddie settled down in Aunt Nellie's sewing room. "I have a few things to show you in my trunk. It just might cheer you up," Aunt Nellie said. "I want y'all to know about what your people doing here in Harlem."

Now Bessie sat up, alert.

Aunt Nellie pulled out a magazine. "Bessie, I bet you ain't never seen a magazine written all by coloreds, have you?"

Bessie shook her head.

Aunt Nellie read a poem from it written by a man named Langston Hughes. "That was written by what they are calling the 'New Negro.' Folks like Langston Hughes are proud to be colored and even outright talk about *liking* to have black skin."

Bessie had never heard a colored person calling somebody "black" unless he was trying to be mean. Now Aunt Nellie was saying the "New Negro" liked being black.

"Here in Harlem, colored people can write poetry, be doctors and architects, sing and dance in clubs, and even be policemen," Aunt Nellie said proudly.

She gathered up a few things from the trunk. "One second," she said. "I'll be right back." When Aunt Nellie returned, she had on a different dress. It was bright yellow and covered with beads and fringe. She spun around so they could see it, and everything on the dress spun with her.

"This is called a flapper dress," Aunt Nellie said. "Have you ever seen anything so beautiful?"

"No, ma'am," Bessie said.

"N-n-not me," said Eddie.

"I used to dance in it at Small's Paradise over on Seventh Avenue," Aunt Nellie said. "That's a fancy nightclub, let me tell you."

"What's a nightclub?" Bessie asked.

"Well, a nightclub is a place where grown folk can dance and laugh and talk together. Sometimes clubs have shows where folk perform—you know, dancing and singing on a stage."

"Are you a d-dancer?" Eddie asked.

"Oh, not really," Aunt Nellie said. "See, when we waited tables we'd dance like this." She put a record on the Victrola and began to swing her hips. "We'd do the Charleston as we sashayed on up to the table. Come on, let me show you how to Charleston."

Aunt Nellie pushed back a coffee table. "Put one of your hands on your hip like this," she said. "Now swing your right leg around behind your left leg. And then give your right foot a little twist and whip it out like so, then swing your left leg behind your right leg. That's it. Y'all got it!" All three of them swirled, pretending to hold a tray up in the air with one hand, as they danced around the floor.

"Small's Paradise is a nice club," Aunt Nellie said, while they pranced back and forth to the music. "Not like the Cotton Club."

"What's the Cotton Club?" Bessie asked, imagining a bunch of people all holding bundles of cotton.

"The Cotton Club is a fancy uptown nightclub where coloreds can perform, but we ain't allowed in to *see* the show."

"Why don't you work for Small's Paradise anymore?" Bessie asked.

"You don't know your Aunt Esther. She still calls me 'Baby Sister,'" Aunt Nellie said. "You ought to be glad she's off to Boston seeing about her daughter. Lord, if she was here you think she'd be letting us listen to what she calls the devil's music? No. And God knows she's worse since her husband, Reverend Henry, died. Much worse. After he died she found out he hadn't paid—" Aunt Nellie stopped dancing. "Where's my mind? I can't talk about that with y'all."

"She found out he hadn't paid what, Aunt Nellie?" Bessie asked. "We're big children, remember? Our secret."

Aunt Nellie glanced nervously at the mantle clock. "Lordy, it's after nine o'clock."

"Please tell us. Please," Bessie begged.

"All right," Aunt Nellie said, sitting down with Bessie and Eddie on the floor. "See, Reverend Henry wasn't allowed to buy this house, because the owners didn't want to sell to coloreds, so he used the down payment to rent the house. But he didn't tell your Aunt Esther because he didn't want to break her—"

Just then Papa walked into the room. Bessie barely recognized him. He looked worn out. And he looked like he was mad about something.

Bessie and Eddie ran to him and wrapped their arms around him. "Hey, Papa," they said together.

"Hey, Bessie and Eddie," Papa said, stooping down to hug them.

"Where you been, Papa?" Bessie asked. In her mind she saw him hugging the woman the night before outside the window. She hoped he would say something that would explain it all. Her heart sank when he answered—with a fib.

"I been getting up early for work and coming in late. I just left work," Papa said, staring at Aunt Nellie.

"W-w-we missed you, Papa," Eddie said.

"I know. I missed y'all, too," Papa said. "Y'all been good like I told you?"

"Yes, sir," Eddie answered. Bessie didn't say anything. Instead she dropped her head and thought to herself, *Have* you *been good, Papa?* She took a long look at Papa. He didn't have on his work clothes, and he was still clean.

Papa was always dirty when he came from work building things and digging wells.

"I'm glad you been good. That's more than I can say for your aunt." Papa straightened up his tall body and looked directly into Aunt Nellie's face. "These children don't need to be hearing nothing like that, Nellie. You don't talk to children about grown folks' burdens, girl. What else you been telling them?"

"I ain't told them nothing," Aunt Nellie said, slinging her stuff back into the trunk. She yanked the record off the Victrola. "Don't come in here accusing me of something I ain't done, Ed Coulter. At least I ain't told Esther what *you* been doing, now have I?"

"I been working," Papa said.

"Yeah. What *kind* of work, though?" Aunt Nellie said, biting her lower lip.

"Work's work. Something *you* ought to think about. Leastways, I ain't let her run me out of doing what I want to be doing. You so scared of her, Nellie, that—" Papa stopped and looked at Bessie and Eddie. "I'm tired," he continued. "Look, I'm sorry, Nellie. I know you doing the best you can. And I appreciate it." Papa slumped down on one of the stuffed chairs.

"Well, just because you tired don't give you no call to say all that. You worse than Esther sometimes," Aunt Nellie said.

Papa broke into a fit of coughing.

"Ed, are you all right?" Aunt Nellie asked, then covered her mouth with her hand.

"All I'm saying is," Papa said, coughing in between breaths, "I done told you, I want both my children in bed before this time of night, Nellie. You done promised me you'd look after them."

Aunt Nellie grabbed Bessie and Eddie by the shoulders. "All right, then." Bending down in front of them, she whispered, "You two go on to bed. You take this, Bessie," she said, slipping a sheet of paper into Bessie's hand.

Bessie looked at the paper as she walked upstairs. It was the poem Aunt Nellie had read. It was called "The Weary Blues." Bessie was so busy reading it that she didn't even realize until she was in the bedroom that Eddie wasn't with her. When she went back downstairs to get him, he was standing outside the sewing room.

Bessie could hear Papa talking. "Ain't no work for a colored man paying no decent money 'round here. That's why I have to spend so much time at the Dark Tower. I'm thinking about moving in there. It's the only way. I've got to get back to her. You see that, don't you? I love her."

Suddenly Papa spun around and saw Bessie and Eddie crouched at the door. "Y'all, didn't I tell you to go up-stairs to bed?"

They raced up to their room.

"What's th-the Tower?" Eddie asked.

"The *Dark* Tower," Bessie said, annoyed that she didn't know either.

"Papa kept s-s-saying he had to go be with this w-woman at the Dark Tower place. Who is th-the w-w-woman?" Eddie asked.

Bessie pulled Eddie to her and hugged him tightly. So it was true. Papa and Mama were separated, and Papa was seeing another woman. There was nothing she could do about Mama now, except hope that Mama was really coming to Harlem. She couldn't even write to Mama, because Mama had never learned to read too well. But maybe Bessie could find out who the woman was that Papa was talking about, and find out about the Dark Tower. Why would Papa want to be in a dark tower? Bessie tried to imagine what it would be like. Cold and wet and gloomy. Spooky, with candles burning. "Don't worry. I'll figure this out," Bessie said.

"H-how?" Eddie asked.

"I don't know yet. I'm thinking. Just don't worry about it," Bessie said. "Remember, I'm your big sister. I'll take care of you."

They took their baths and got in bed. Once again, Papa didn't come in to say good night. He hadn't been in to say good night since their first night in Harlem. Bessie lay awake thinking about what she must do to find out what Papa was up to. Why was he acting like this? Eddie

snored lightly beside her. Bessie turned over and pulled
out the poem Aunt Nellie had given her. By the light of
the moon, she read a few lines:

> *In a deep song voice with a melancholy tone*
> *I heard that Negro sing, that old piano moan—*
> *"Ain't got nobody in all this world,*
> *Ain't got nobody but ma self."*

Even though there were parts of the poem she didn't
understand, the words touched her heart. She felt like she,
too, had nobody in the world to help her. But she was
determined to find out what Papa was doing.

Bessie heard a noise in the hallway. What was it? She
listened to see if it was Papa finally coming to say good
night. But their door didn't swing open.

Bessie threw the covers back and sneaked to the
door. She slowly turned the knob and peered out. In the
dimness she saw Papa walking down the hall. He had his
good shoes in his hands. He had changed into his Sunday
church clothes, gray pants and his white starched shirt.
His suspenders were the black and white ones that Mama
had bought him for his birthday last year. He tiptoed into
the bathroom and closed the door softly.

Papa must be going out. Was he going to the Dark
Tower? It would be useless to ask him. He wouldn't tell
her, and he'd already warned Aunt Nellie about telling

them grown folks' business. Bessie closed the door quietly. There was only one way to find out about this Dark Tower—follow Papa there.

Bessie hurriedly slipped on her clothes. She waited at the door of her room. Her heart beat like Brownie's hooves when the mare was at full gallop. It thumped so loudly, Bessie feared Papa would hear it when he sneaked past her door and down the stairs.

Bessie waited until she heard Papa go out the front door. She moved quietly down the stairs and out the door. Bessie could see Papa up ahead, turning the corner. Bessie knew she needed to stay far enough behind that Papa didn't hear or see her. She followed him, trying to keep her steps light on the pavement.

After a few blocks, the smell of turnips and pork chops drifted out of an apartment building. Three men hopped out of a car.

"Hurry up, man. We're late for jooking," one man said. They were dressed in black suits, white shirts, and black bow ties and carried black horn cases. Papa stopped and talked to the men as if he knew them. Papa's friends back home were all farmers and laborers, like Papa.

Two ladies in high-heeled shoes with lots of lipstick and big jangling earrings stopped and talked to Papa. One woman hugged him around the neck. Bessie heard her say, "I hears you been painting uptown." Bessie knew what "painting the town" meant—having fun. Papa ought to be ashamed of himself. What would Mama think? Mama was back home alone, and Papa was painting up the town in Harlem.

For the first time, Bessie was glad Mama wasn't here to see how Papa was acting. Then it came to her that if Mama were here, maybe Papa wouldn't be doing this. She had to stop Papa from seeing other women. If Papa had another woman, Mama might not take him back.

Another man came up and grabbed Papa. They laughed and slapped each other on the back. The man gave Papa a brown paper sack. "I hated to make you come down here for this, but I needed to get out myself," the man said. "I did you a special favor, though—there are two of each for you. You can stow away some for yourself."

"I'll have to hide one set at home," Papa said. "I'm keeping this a secret from my family."

"Come on into the rent party for a minute," the man said, slapping Papa's back again. "You ain't got to stay long. I know you dying to get back to that Tower. But you deserve a break, man."

This isn't the Dark Tower, Bessie thought. Then where were they? And what was in that bag that Papa was keeping a secret?

Bessie watched Papa stop by the door next to a fancy-dressed woman smoking a long cigarette. He gave her something out of his pocket and went up the steps. Bessie could see other people crowding up the steps, too.

Bessie waited until no one but the woman was standing on the steps. She wanted to get a better look at the sign hanging by the door. Maybe it would help her figure out what Papa was up to in there.

Bessie walked briskly toward the building. She read the sign: *RENT PARTY. Only 10¢. Live pick-up trio. Boiled pig's feet, hopping John, ham hocks, and sweet potato pie. Come on in and swing.*

The cigarette woman waved Bessie over to her. One of the apartment windows upstairs had a red light glowing from it. Loud jazz music filled the air. Through the window, Bessie could see people dancing and hear their laughter ringing like bells from above.

"You want to come in to the rent party, miss?" the woman shouted. Her speech was slurred, and smoke curled out of her mouth. "Come on. Help a body get up their rent. You know these landlords is raising rents so high, every dime counts. Landlords'll kick us out if we don't make some money here tonight to pay our rent. Come on, now. Help a sister out. You can dance all you want. Eat all you want."

Bessie figured the woman must have been drinking spirits, the way she swayed and slurred her words.

"It's just a dime to get in," the woman continued, grabbing Bessie by the arm. "We got a live band. Can't you hear it?" Then the woman looked at Bessie, as if seeing her for the first time. "Why, you just a little girl. Go on. Get on out of here and go home. Ain't no children allowed in here," she said, turning Bessie's arm loose.

Bessie backed away from the woman. She didn't want any more trouble than she already had. Bessie hadn't followed Papa to the Dark Tower, but to a party. What had come over Papa? He never did things like this. Back home Papa was a hardworking man. He came home every night. Bessie had never seen Papa even look at another woman. Whatever happened to Papa must have happened here in Harlem. And Bessie would bet a plug nickel that the Dark Tower woman had something to do with it.

CHAPTER 4

WEARY BLUES

essie started for home. Her chest
B tightened. She'd never been so far
from home at night. The normally busy
street was quiet and still. What if she
got lost? Bessie tried to retrace her
steps, but the streets seemed darker
than when she'd followed Papa.

The shadows from the streetlights
played tricks with her eyes. Did she see someone move
up ahead? She ducked into an alley. It smelled of rotting
food. Bessie felt something on her foot and glanced down.
A mouse sat on her shoe. She kicked her foot, trying to
shake the mouse off. "Go on," she whispered. "Git off.
Go. Git." Bessie wasn't afraid of the mouse. She'd had
field mice for pets back home. The mouse looked at her
bravely, then scurried away. The sight of the fearless
little creature made Bessie feel braver. She touched her
Memaw necklace for courage and started out again,
hurrying home as fast as she could.

Bessie sighed with relief as she sneaked back into her aunts' house. Upstairs, she found Eddie sound asleep. But Bessie couldn't sleep. What in the world was happening to Papa? Had he forgotten about Mama already?

A pang of hurt passed through Bessie. What about *her*? Didn't she sometimes forget about Mama when she was playing? Was she just as bad as Papa?

Bessie decided to stay awake and listen for Papa to come back home. But the next morning, she woke with a start. She realized she'd dozed off to sleep. Had Papa come home last night? Bessie raced to his room and flung the door open.

"What's the matter?" Aunt Nellie asked, coming up the stairs. "You need something?"

"No, ma'am," Bessie said. But it wasn't true—she needed Papa. Not this new Papa, but the old Papa who loved his children and Mama. "I was looking for Papa," Bessie said. "Is he downstairs?"

"No. I mean, your papa, well, he . . . he left early to go to work," Aunt Nellie said, tugging at her ear. "He had to go back to work last night and he came in real late. And then he had to get up early this morning and leave again. Yes, that's right."

Bessie stared at her. Aunt Nellie wasn't a very good fibber, that was for sure.

"Come on down and get your breakfast. I've made you and Eddie some hotcakes and homemade syrup.

Hurry up, now. You don't want the cakes to get cold,"
she said, leaving Bessie alone in Papa's room.

Bessie leaned against the door and thought about
what Aunt Nellie had said. That was the same story
Aunt Nellie told them every time they asked for Papa.
Suppose he went out every night the way he did last
night. Maybe that's why he had stopped coming in to
say good night. Suppose he stayed out all night at parties.
Bessie looked around Papa's room. His bed sure didn't
look slept in. How could she know whether or not Papa
even slept here?

Bessie had an idea. She pulled at a loose string near the
top of the bedspread. Leaving one end of the string connected to the bedspread, she tied the other end to the
nearest leg of the bed. If the string was broken tomorrow,
Bessie would know that Papa had pulled the spread back
to get into bed. Bessie hoped that string would be broken
the next time she checked.

The next morning, right after breakfast, Bessie
hurried into Papa's bedroom. Her string was still there
in one piece. According to Aunt Nellie, Papa had once
again come home after they were asleep and left early
in the morning. Bessie liked Aunt Nellie and knew she
meant well. But Aunt Nellie was fibbing for Papa.

Now Bessie knew Papa wasn't *sleeping* at home. But was he coming home at all? For two nights Bessie tried tricks to stay awake so she would hear if Papa came in. But it was hard to stay awake. Back home, Bessie was in the habit of going to bed with the chickens around seven o'clock. That way she got plenty of rest before Mama called her at dawn to do chores.

Last night she had fallen asleep before ten o'clock. Now it was ten-thirty, and Bessie was struggling to keep her eyes open. She tried not to think about Mama and Papa, because it made her sad. But she couldn't help thinking about home.

She thought about a day several weeks before they left Burlington. It was soon after Bessie had noticed Mama's unhappiness. Bessie had been sitting on the floor between Mama's legs while Mama combed, greased, and plaited Bessie's hair. "Bessie," she had said softly, "I love fixing your hair. I think it's what I will miss the most."

Mama had been giving clues all along, and Bessie had missed them. Now she could see that it all added up. Papa not saying his sugar-sweets. Mama saying she would miss combing Bessie's hair. Mama giving her Memaw's necklace. Yes, Mama knew that she and Papa were going to separate and that Papa would take them to Harlem. Those were her ways of saying good-bye. But why would Papa tell a fib and say that Mama was coming to Harlem? Bessie had never known Papa to fib before.

People change, though. Bessie knew that. *She'd* changed. Since coming to Harlem, she'd almost forgotten Brownie. Back home she'd ridden her horse every day. She'd wake up thinking about that horse. Now she went days without thinking about her. Or about the starry sky in her room. What if she forgot Mama? There could be nothing worse than to forget your own mama.

Bessie felt so alone. She couldn't tell Eddie everything she knew. He wouldn't understand. But she would tell him just enough so he could help. She whispered some lines from Mr. Hughes's poem. *Ain't got nobody in all this world. Ain't got nobody but ma self.* Now Bessie felt like she knew what that meant as she whispered the poem into the night. She was surely having the weary blues in Harlem.

Early the next morning, Bessie and Eddie sat outside on the stoop.

"Eddie, I don't think Papa is coming home at night," Bessie said.

"Aunt Nellie s-s-says he leaves early," Eddie said. "And we g-go to bed b-b-before he gets in, that's all."

"I don't think so, Eddie. Papa ain't doing right."

Eddie shook his head. " P-p-papa w-wouldn't do wrong, Bessie."

"I followed Papa, Eddie, and . . ." Bessie saw the pain creeping up on Eddie's face.

"A-a-and w-w-what?" he asked her.

She couldn't do it. She couldn't tell him Papa was hugging a woman the other night. And that when she'd followed him to a party he was hugging other women, too. Eddie was too young to be hurt like that.

"Eddie," Bessie said. "I don't think Mama is really coming to Harlem. I think Papa and Mama are separated. And you know that lady at the Dark Tower? I think Papa is spending all his time with her. I need you to help me find out where this Dark Tower is and who the woman is."

Eddie didn't move. Bessie couldn't tell what he was thinking or feeling. Was she going to have to do this all alone?

Then Bessie heard the clicking of a door behind them. It was Lillian.

"May I sit with you, please?" Lillian asked, as she closed the door behind her.

Bessie wanted to say no. This was private between her and Eddie. But there was something about Lillian that made Bessie feel sorry for her. Maybe it was because she didn't have any friends. "Come on. You can sit down," Bessie said.

"Thank you very much," Lillian said. "My mother says that if it is all right with your father, you can come over to supper. If he is back, I will wait here until you ask him."

Bessie couldn't hold back her tears. She knew crying wasn't going to help, but the mention of Papa made her hurt so badly inside.

"What did I say?" Lillian asked. "I'm sorry. Did something happen to your papa?"

Bessie wiped her eyes. She couldn't cry every time someone mentioned Papa.

"I saw your father leaving this morning, early," Lillian said. "He was dressed up, and he had a small black satchel with him. Was the woman who picked him up your mother?"

Bessie stared at Lillian. "What woman? Have you ever seen her before?" Bessie asked.

"No," Lillian said, "I have never seen her. But she was pretty. And she looked like she was very rich."

"Sh-sh-she is not our m-m-m-mama," Eddie said loudly. Now he was crying.

Lillian reached into the small beaded purse she carried and handed them each a lace handkerchief. "I'm sorry I made you cry. If it's not your mother, who is it?"

Bessie wished Lillian would go away. She was embarrassed that Lillian had seen her papa with the woman who was taking him away from his family.

Eddie blurted out, "It's P-p-papa's g-g-girlfriend."

"Eddie!" Bessie said sharply. She couldn't believe Eddie would say that out loud. Sure, that's what Bessie had meant when she said Papa was with another woman. But she didn't want to hear anyone *say* it. She was sure Lillian wouldn't want anything to do with them now.

"I am sorry. Really, I am," Lillian said. "Is there anything I can do to help?"

"Really?" Bessie asked. "You still want to be our friend?"

"Of course," Lillian said. Bessie knew then that Lillian could be trusted.

"Do you think you can help us find the woman you saw picking my papa up?" Bessie asked. "If I find her, maybe I can find my papa. I saw him outside with a woman one night. She was very tall." Bessie still could not bring herself to tell them that she had seen Papa hugging the woman.

"I bet it's the same woman," Lillian said. "Was she in a black automobile?"

"Yes! It was shiny, with a lot of silver things on it," Bessie said. "I couldn't see her that well, though."

"When I saw her, she had on a lot of diamonds and gold, with a mink stole over her shoulder," Lillian said excitedly. "She must be very rich. Do you know anything else about the woman?"

"No, except that she spends time at a place called the Dark Tower," Bessie said. "Sometimes she and Papa must stay there. Papa pretends to go to work, but he's really spending time with that woman. Do you want to help us find her?"

"I'd be honored," Lillian said.

"You're a really good friend, Lillian," Bessie said.

A look of happiness sprang up on Lillian's face. Bessie realized it must have been tough for Lillian to be in a strange place for three years without friends.

"*Best* friends?" Lillian asked.

"You promise you won't tell anyone about Papa?" Bessie asked.

"Not anyone," Lillian said. "I promise."

"Then, yes, we can be best friends. Let's cross on it," Bessie said.

"Splendid." Lillian held out her pinkie.

"I-I-I'll cross, too," Eddie said. They all three linked their pinkies and made a vow of secrecy. *Lillian is the strangest-talking best friend I've ever had,* Bessie thought. But it felt good to find a friend in Harlem.

CHAPTER 5

CAUGHT

I'm gonna sneak into Papa's room," Bessie said after she and Eddie had gone back inside. "Maybe he has something in there that will help us figure out who the woman is. I need you to be a lookout." Bessie knew that if Papa caught her in his room going through his private things, he would be madder than a raccoon caught in a trap. And Bessie would surely get a whipping.

"Stay right outside," Bessie said. "And if you hear anyone coming up the stairs, just open the door real quiet-like and whisper to me."

Bessie sneaked into the room. She gave one last look to Eddie stretched out on the landing, peering down over the banister. "Stay alert," she whispered.

Inside Papa's room, Bessie panicked. It didn't feel right to be going through Papa's personal things. But she needed to know what he was up to.

Bessie looked around the room. The bed was just as Bessie had left it, the string in place, unbroken, and the bedspread hanging crooked. If Papa did come home last night, he must have just changed his clothes and gone right back out.

A pair of Papa's work pants were folded on a chair near the door. His work boots were sitting at the foot of the bed. Papa never did any work without those brogans on. There was no chifforobe in this room, so Papa kept his clothes in a suitcase. Bessie dragged the suitcase from behind the bed and opened it.

She sat on the floor and started taking things out, one at a time. On top were Papa's clean work clothes. Bessie knew every piece of Papa's and Mama's clothes. One of her chores back home was to help Mama on wash day. She stirred the clothes in the washtub for Mama, and she helped Mama pin the clothes on the wire clotheslines Papa had put up between the house and the barn. Bessie loved helping Mama on wash day. It made her feel more grown up.

A few of the shirts in Papa's suitcase were speckled with paint. Bessie picked up a white shirt. There were paint spots on it, too. Bessie couldn't remember Papa painting anything around the house with the colors on the shirt. She smelled the shirts. They were Papa's, all right. He always smelled spicy like cinnamon water, a mixture he made for himself.

Bessie pulled out a brown paper bag. Her hand shook as she lifted it from the suitcase. It looked like the bag that man had handed Papa at the rent party—Papa's secret.

Bessie emptied the contents onto the floor in front of her. Eight small tins spilled out. Bessie opened one. She smelled it. It was just some kind of paint. There were also a few different-sized paintbrushes. They didn't look like Papa's, though. Papa's paintbrushes back home were either big bulky things or plain wood-handled brushes. These were as small as pencils. Bessie picked one up. The brushes were attached to pretty wood handles with gold engraved bands.

Bessie tapped one of the paintbrushes on the suitcase as she thought. Why did the man give these to Papa? And what kind of secret could this be? Paint and paintbrushes? It didn't make sense.

Bessie's eyes wandered back to the suitcase. She spotted a gold envelope sticking out between some shirts. Two words were written on the front of the envelope—*Dark Tower.* Her fingers trembled as she slid the envelope out. She opened the flap and pulled out a thin sheet of notepaper.

Bessie swallowed hard. Did she dare read Papa's mail? She had to—maybe it held the answer to where Papa was. As she read the note, her breath left her body like a bird swooping away.

Dear Ed,
  Glad you've taken my advice about staying with me
at the Tower. It'll make things much easier for us.
                                    Love,
                                    A.

Bessie felt sick. Here was the proof that Papa had left
them for the woman at the Dark Tower. How could this
happen? Bessie squeezed the note in her hand. Every part
of her body felt like it was on fire. How could Papa do this
to Mama? It wasn't right. And it wasn't like Papa.

Bessie felt so mad at Papa it hurt. Then suddenly it
came to her that maybe it wasn't all Papa's fault. Papa
wouldn't just walk off and leave his children, would he?
Didn't he bring Bessie and Eddie with him to Harlem?
No, the only way Papa would do something like this was
if someone put a conjure on him. Bessie knew she needed
to find this Miss A. woman and break her spell.

Bessie stuffed the note from Miss A. into her pocket.
She had just begun folding everything back into the suitcase when the door creaked open.

Bessie jumped up.

"B-B-Bessie—" Eddie said, peeping inside, alarm on
his face.

It was too late. Bessie could hear footsteps at the top
of the stairs. She quickly pulled Eddie into the room. She
flung the last shirt into the suitcase.

The footsteps were outside the door. Bessie expected the door to fly open any second. She pushed Eddie under the bed and scooted after him. Bessie pulled the bedspread down so it hid them from sight. But the footsteps continued on past Papa's room.

Bessie cupped her hand over Eddie's ear so her whisper wouldn't carry. "Was it Papa?"

"I-I-I d-d-don't know," Eddie whispered back to her.

"Shhhhh," Bessie said as she heard the door of Papa's room squeak open.

The footsteps moved to where Bessie had left the suitcase. She swallowed. She had been in such a hurry, she had forgotten to close the suitcase and stand it back against the wall behind the bed.

Bessie heard the sound of the suitcase lid thudding shut. Then the tapping of a foot. The footsteps came closer and closer to the bed. Bessie wished she had left enough room between the bedspread's hem and the floor so she could peep out. Did she dare lift the bedspread up?

Then Bessie felt Eddie shifting behind her. Not a lot, but enough to hear the swishing sound of his pajamas on the hardwood floor. Bessie couldn't risk moving to signal him to be still. She squeezed her eyes shut and prayed that if it was Papa, he wouldn't hear. Bessie could hear the person's shallow breathing. Whoever it was was still in the room. But the person hadn't moved for a while.

Bessie wished she could see what was happening.

The footsteps sounded again, heading for the door. Bessie heard the door creaking, and then shutting. She breathed a sigh of relief. Finally she and Eddie could sneak back into their room.

"*Achoo. Aaaaaaachhooooo,*" Eddie sneezed. "I-I-I'm sorry," he quickly whispered.

The door opened again. *Boom, boom, boom.* Three steps and the person was at the bedspread. Bessie could barely make out a shadow, but it had to be Papa. Aunt Nellie wouldn't walk across the room in three giant steps. *Oh, no,* Bessie thought. Maybe she should peep out now to see. But it was too late. A wrinkled brown hand lifted up the bedspread.

Bessie stared at thick-soled black shoes. Then her eyes followed the trail to the bulky brown stockings tied in a knot just below the knees.

"Just what are you two doing under that bed?" the woman said. "Get out from under there this minute! You don't belong in here."

Bessie crawled out. Eddie followed. It was Aunt Esther. Bessie had seen her at Grandma's funeral, bossing everyone around.

"Look at you children with all that dust on you. What are you doing snooping in this room, anyway?"

"Good morning, Aunt Esther," Bessie said, dusting her clothes off.

"Baby Sister, get up here right now," Aunt Esther shouted, ignoring Bessie.

"W-w-we were cleaning under th-th-the b-b-bed," Eddie said, looking like he'd eaten a mouse.

"You what? Don't tell lies, boy. I can't abide liars in my house. And why are you stuttering so terribly? Slow down, and you can talk clearer."

"We're sorry, Aunt Esther," Bessie said. "Eddie was just making a joke."

Aunt Nellie walked in. She looked different—tired. "Yes, what is it?" she asked Aunt Esther.

"I want to know why these children were hiding under Little Ed's bed. And I want to know why you haven't helped this boy stop his stuttering. You know I can't abide a person who can't speak plainly."

"Maybe you just make him nervous," Aunt Nellie said. She looked like she knew what the weary blues were, too, Bessie thought.

"Well, right now I want to know why you allowed these children to be snooping all over my house."

Aunt Nellie tugged her ear. "I told them to hide under the bed to surprise their papa when he came back."

Bessie closed her eyes. Aunt Nellie couldn't fib at all. She was worse than Eddie. Who was going to believe that a grown-up sent them under the bed to surprise Papa?

"You did, did you? Uh-huh," Aunt Esther said. "Well, all this nonsense is going to stop. And look at all that dust that was under the bed. Nellie, all I ask in exchange for you staying here is to help keep the house clean. You know I don't abide dust."

"Esther, why don't you let the children go get ready for breakfast?" Aunt Nellie said, sighing.

"Don't tell me what to do in my house, Baby Sister," Aunt Esther said. "No wonder Little Ed wanted me here. I told him you would let the children run all over you." She turned to Bessie and Eddie. "You children are out of control. Get downstairs right now. I'll deal with you in a minute."

Bessie shivered. She felt like the coldest freeze of winter was inside her body. She imagined she was the tobacco when the ice takes it over, turning it dry and not fit for use. She couldn't believe it, but Aunt Esther must be worse than Mama and Papa about not letting you grow up. She still called Papa "Little Ed." Even Grandma hadn't called him that.

Downstairs at breakfast, Aunt Esther served them something white that sort of looked like grits. "Aunt Esther," Bessie asked, "what is this?"

Aunt Esther stopped scrubbing the counter and turned to stare at Bessie. "What *is* it? Girl, what have you been eating for breakfast?"

Eddie spoke up. "B-b-bacon and s-s-sausage and stuff."

"Bacon? Sausage? Lord, that girl knows how expensive

meat is. That's rich folks' eating. What in the world else did you eat?"

Now Bessie was sorry she'd asked the question. She might get Aunt Nellie in trouble. "It's all right," Bessie said. "We ate this. I just forgot what it's called."

"Uh-huh," Aunt Esther said, eyeing Bessie like she didn't believe a word of it. "It's Cream of Wheat. It's healthy and it's cheap. I can't believe Baby Sister would be giving you children meat every day like we got money to burn. She's going to put me in the poorhouse."

Bessie watched Aunt Esther mumbling around the kitchen. She and Eddie ate the strange cereal in silence. Finally, Aunt Esther sat down at the table. "I have something to tell you children. Your papa had to leave. He's gone away to work for a while. He'll be back, though. Don't worry. He wired me to come home so I could take care of you. Now that I'm here, you children will be taken care of the way you ought to be."

Bessie didn't lower her spoon from her mouth. She felt like she would cry any second.

Aunt Esther reached over and patted Bessie's other hand. "Now, now, you two don't get upset. It'll be all right. I'm going to be right here."

"I-I-I-I-I w-w-want M-m-mama," Eddie said.

Bessie dropped the spoon into her bowl and took his hand in hers. "Don't cry, please," she pleaded, shifting her eyes to Aunt Esther.

"It ain't no need to be crying, boy," Aunt Esther said. "I raised Baby Sister and your papa when our mama was away working as a live-in maid. And they both turned out all right. What you crying for?"

Now Eddie sniffled and rubbed his eyes. "B-B-Bessie, I-I-I-I w-want Mama *now*."

"Don't cry. Mama will be here soon. Papa said so," Bessie reassured him, hoping that what she was saying was the truth.

"Children, there ain't no reason for you to start acting up. Even if your mama or papa doesn't come, I'm going to take good care of you."

Aunt Esther's words cut Bessie's heart like a knife. Mama might not come. True, Bessie had thought to herself that Mama and Papa were separated, but she didn't really believe that it was for good. And she never considered that the Dark Tower woman could take Papa from her and Eddie. Mama and Papa both gone—neither of them ever coming back? It couldn't be.

Bessie jumped up from the table. "I want to know when Mama is coming," Bessie demanded. She didn't care if Aunt Esther scolded her. "And where is Papa working, Aunt Esther?"

"First of all, don't take that tone with me, girl," Aunt Esther said.

Bessie wanted to take a different tone. She didn't want to sound disrespectful, but she couldn't help it.

She felt light-headed and unsteady on her feet. She wanted to scream, *Where's Mama and Papa?* She felt her body trembling all over, like leaves in a storm. She clenched her fists tightly at her sides. Her breath came quick and short.

"Girl, you better sit down," Aunt Esther said, standing up and walking to the sink. "What's gotten into you? I told you, your papa is away working, and that's all you need to know. Now, here," she said, turning and handing them a brown bottle and two rags.

Bessie didn't flinch. She glared at the bottle and rags. "Aunt Esther, when is Mama coming to be with us in Harlem? When is Papa coming back?" she asked again. But this time Bessie was so close to crying, the words came out like a whisper of wind in the trees.

Aunt Esther acted as though she didn't even hear her question now. "Don't tell me that Baby Sister didn't make you do your chores. You're to polish the furniture in the sitting room every morning. And then you can go outside for a stretch and play. But don't go off this block."

Aunt Esther set the bottle and rags down on the table. "You won't go out until it's done. It's up to you how long you're inside." Then she walked out, leaving them standing in the room.

"B-B-Bessie, the quicker we d-d-dust, the faster we can g-go outside. I want to g-g-get out of here," Eddie said.

"You're right," Bessie said. "We need to go out so we can talk and come up with a plan. We can't let Papa stay with that woman in the Dark Tower. If we do, then we won't have anyone."

CHAPTER 6
HALF-TRUTHS

It took three inspections before Aunt Esther could see her reflection in the furniture and allowed Bessie and Eddie to go outside. Once they were settled on the stoop, Bessie reached into her dress pocket and pulled out the note from Miss A. that she had found in Papa's suitcase. Bessie *had* to discover where the Dark Tower was and find this woman. There was no doubt in her mind that Miss A. had put some kind of spell on Papa to make him act the way he was acting.

"Eddie, I have a note from the woman Papa likes. I need you to help me figure out how to find her," Bessie said. She was just showing the crumpled note to Eddie when Lillian walked out on the stoop. Bessie slipped the note back into her pocket.

"B-B-Bessie f-found a note," Eddie blurted out.

Bessie gave Eddie a stern look. She didn't want Lillian

to read the note. Even though Lillian was supposed to help them, Bessie felt embarrassed by a woman writing to Papa.

"Where is the note?" Lillian asked.

Bessie looked at her friend. Lillian *had* said that she'd help, and she did already know about the woman. She'd even seen the woman's face. And if they were going to look for Miss A., Lillian knew her way around Harlem better than Bessie and Eddie did.

"Here it is," Bessie said, pulling the note out and showing it to Lillian.

"See," Lillian said, "I told you, she's very rich. This is real gold around the edges of the note. Those leaf patterns on the border are gold, too. And that's engraving there at the top where the initials are."

Bessie looked at the fancy engraved letters. "Her initials must be A.W. Now all we have to do is find her," Bessie said. "Or find out where that Dark Tower is."

"How?" Lillian asked.

"Well, maybe we could walk around the neighborhood and ask people if they know a rich woman with the initials A.W.," Bessie said.

"H-how can we g-get away from Aunt Esther?" Eddie said.

"Your other aunt is back?" Lillian asked. "Oh, no."

"Yes," Bessie said. "She must have come back last night sometime. And she's very strict. She told us not to leave the block."

"I think I have an idea to help you get away. If it works, I'll see you after lunch," Lillian said, getting up to go back inside. "I must start working on Mother."

Bessie and Eddie ate their lunch in silence. Aunt Esther had cooked them some collard greens and rice. Bessie loved collard greens, but she didn't feel much like eating. She wondered what Lillian had meant by "working on Mother."

When they were almost finished eating, the sound of the door knocker echoed through the house. Aunt Esther stopped stringing beans and went to the door. Bessie and Eddie snuck just far enough into the hallway to see who was at the door. They were surprised to hear Lillian's mother talking to Aunt Esther.

As soon as Aunt Esther closed the door, she called Bessie and Eddie. "You children didn't tell me you'd made such an impressive friend," Aunt Esther said. "Lillian Moore's mother came over herself to ask if you would go with Lillian to her uncle's bookstore. I told her you would love to do that. Richard Moore is a respected businessman. Go on now. Hurry and wash up. Don't keep Lillian waiting."

By the time they got out to the stoop, Lillian was already there.

"Thanks, Lillian. Good work," Bessie said.

"Let's go. We don't have much time," Lillian said. "I have to be back by supper."

They walked up the street and turned the corner.

"Who should we ask about Miss A.W. first?" Lillian asked.

"Ask th-that lady," Eddie said, pointing to a woman just leaving the butcher shop. "Aunt Esther says that in Harlem only r-r-rich p-people eat a lot of meat."

They walked over to the butcher shop. The sign in the window read, "Pig's Feet, Pig Snout, Hog Mawls, and Chitlins." Bessie's mouth watered—it reminded her of the good food back home.

"Excuse me, ma'am," Bessie said. "Do you know a rich colored woman who has the initials A.W.?" The woman shook her head no and turned down the sidewalk.

Next Lillian asked the shoe-shine man. "Sir, may I bother you to inquire about a woman? Do you happen to know a rich colored woman with a fancy black car?"

"Girl, if I had me a frail-eel like that, don't you know, me and her would be on the first thing smoking," the old man said.

"Excuse me, sir, but I don't understand," Lillian said, frowning.

"Come on, Lillian," Bessie said, pulling her away.

"What did he say?" Lillian asked as they walked down the street.

"I think he was saying if he had a pretty woman like that, he'd take her away from Harlem," Bessie said.

"How do you know that's what he said?" Lillian asked.

"I guessed," Bessie said, smiling for the first time in a while. They made a good team. Lillian had the book smarts, and Bessie and Eddie had the everyday smarts.

They continued several blocks, asking people about the woman. Finally they were almost at the corner where Lillian's uncle had a bookstore.

"Do you think any of the books in your uncle's store can help us?" Bessie asked.

"They might," Lillian said as they stepped up on the curb. Suddenly Lillian grabbed Bessie and Eddie and pulled them down behind a truck. "Wait," she said. "I think we have a problem." Lillian peered out from around the truck. "Yes. It is my father's car. He is visiting with my uncle. We can't go in there now. My father will surely offer to drive us back home."

"Then what should we do?" asked Bessie. "I'm not going back until I find out about Miss A.W."

"Why d-d-don't we go on the other s-side of the street and sneak p-p-past your uncle's store?" Eddie said. "Then we can ask m-m-more p-people in the next block."

Bessie was disappointed that they couldn't go inside the bookstore. She had never been inside a place full of books before.

In the next block, Bessie stopped to read a flyer
posted on a storefront window. "Hey, look," Bessie said.
"Maybe this has something to do with Miss A.W. and
Papa."

Lillian joined her and began to read the flyer out loud.

The 135th Street New York Branch Library
proudly presents Countee Cullen, winner of the
Harmon Foundation Gold Medal Award and other
prizes. He will be reading his poems "The Ballad
of the Brown Girl" and "Copper Sun." Cullen is
also the assistant editor of Opportunity: A Journal
of Negro Life—

Lillian stopped reading and shrugged. "It's just a flyer
about a poet reading at the library."

"Yes," Bessie said, "but see here in the smaller print
where the page is torn? It says, 'His own Dark Tow—'
I bet that would spell *Dark Tower.* What else could it spell?
Maybe this Cullen man owns the Dark Tower where Papa
and Miss A.W. are staying."

"You could be right. We could go to the 135th Street
public library now and ask someone," Lillian said.

"But *we* can't go there," Bessie said.

"Sure we can," Lillian said. "It is not that far. We can
walk there long before it's closed."

"I mean coloreds can't go in the library," Bessie said.

"Of course we can," Lillian said. "Why wouldn't we be able to go in?"

"In the South, colored people can only go into libraries to clean," Bessie explained.

"Well, in Harlem you can go in and read. Now come on," Lillian said.

⌒⊃

When Bessie walked into the 135th Street New York Branch Library, she felt as though she were walking into a wondrous dream. Everywhere she looked she saw books. Books on shelves. Books on tables. Glass cases with books in them. A few people sat reading at long tables. Posters of books and framed pictures of colored people were on the walls. Bessie could never have imagined this back in Burlington—that one day she, Bessie Carol Coulter, would be standing in a library filled with books.

The hush of the room was like a silent song to Bessie. Only in North Carolina, lazing on the banks of a stream, had she felt such peace and serenity. Bessie felt like this was the kind of place she could stay in forever. A place to go when nothing else was right.

"Look," said Lillian, pointing to a case. "These books were written by colored people from all over the world."

"I don't believe it," Bessie said. "That ain't true. Colored people ain't write this many books."

Lillian pulled Bessie over to a shelf. "These are all newspapers by coloreds. See this book, that book, those over there? All written by colored men and women."

Bessie looked in one book after another. She sat at a table flipping through the pages of the newspapers. She read some of the headlines, amazed to find stories about colored people on all the pages. The papers talked about all kinds of things having to do with colored people. There were names like W. E. B. Du Bois and Paul Robeson and information about The National Association for the Advancement of Colored People. Bessie read many other names that Aunt Nellie had mentioned. And there were lots of things written about rich colored people.

Bessie was sure now that she could find information about Miss A.W. right here in this library. Bessie searched through old issues of magazines for any sign of Miss A.W.

Bessie picked up the issue of *Opportunity* from May 1925 and found a wonderful surprise. Right there in its pages was Mr. Langston Hughes's poem "The Weary Blues," awarded first prize in a poetry contest. Bessie could not help grinning. For a second this made her forget all about Miss A.W. and the Dark Tower.

Lillian came over and said, "What are you smiling about?"

"Nothing," Bessie said, feeling guilty.

"I'm looking over there," Lillian said, pointing to a stack of books. "But it's getting late. We have to hurry."

"I'll hurry. Where's Eddie?" Bessie asked.

"He's over there reading old copies of *The Brownie's Book*," Lillian said, pointing. "That's a magazine for colored children."

Bessie began reading again, feeling like there just wasn't enough time to look in all these books, magazines, and newspapers. She opened a newspaper, flipped a few pages, and froze. In the center of the page was a photograph of a beautiful woman. And underneath the photograph was the name A'Lelia Walker. A.W.! But was it *the* woman? Bessie hadn't seen her face very clearly, only her silhouette under the street lamp. Was it just a coincidence that this woman's initials were A.W.? No, it had to be her.

"Come here," Bessie called to Lillian and Eddie. When they rushed over, Bessie excitedly pointed to the photograph. "Look!"

"Shhhhh," said a woman behind a desk.

Bessie took a deep breath. Her heart raced as her voice squeezed out, "Lillian, is this the woman you saw with Papa?"

Lillian studied the photograph. "Yes, that's the woman," she said.

"D-does it s-s-say anything about the Dark Tower, Bessie?" Eddie asked.

"It doesn't say anything about that in this paper. I looked through some other papers, but I didn't see anything else about it," Bessie said.

"You could ask the librarian," Lillian said.

Bessie walked over to the woman who had shushed her. "Ma'am," Bessie said. "Do you know where Mr. Countee Cullen's Dark Tower is?"

The woman pushed wire-rimmed glasses up on her nose. "Why, yes," she said. "Follow me and I'll show you, children."

Bessie, Eddie, and Lillian gave each other excited looks. This was going to be easier than they had thought! But was she going to walk with them all the way to the Tower?

Suddenly Bessie hesitated. She wasn't sure she was ready to come face-to-face with Miss A.W. and Papa. What would she say? What if Papa got really mad at her? What if he got so mad he *never* came back? Bessie shoved these thoughts from her mind. She had to find Miss A.W. at the Dark Tower and break her spell.

They marched behind the librarian to the other side of the room, where there was a tiered wooden rack. "Here, start with this one," the librarian said, passing Bessie an issue of *Opportunity*.

"Where is it?" Bessie asked, taking the magazine. "You mean the address for the Dark Tower is in here?"

"Let me see. I'll look it up for you," the librarian said, taking the magazine from Bessie's hand and flipping rapidly through the pages. "Here you are. Right there." She pointed to a page.

Bessie took the magazine and held it up. She frowned. There was nothing there to help them. "How do we get there, though?" Bessie asked.

"Get there? Here it is. Look," the librarian said, pointing to a section of the magazine. "See, right there. It's Countee Cullen's column, 'The Dark Tower.' You do know what it is, don't you? It's a column that Mr. Cullen writes where he discusses the literature of Negroes. I suspect you might not understand all of it because it's written for adults."

Bessie felt sick to her stomach. Was the Dark Tower a magazine column, not a place? *All this trouble for nothing,* Bessie thought. This was a dead end. So what if she had found the picture of the woman? They were no closer to finding her than before.

"Thank you, ma'am," Bessie said. Then she turned to Lillian and Eddie. "Come on, let's go," she said.

"I'm sorry," Lillian said, looking as sad as Bessie.

"We c-c-could look some m-more."

"I just want to go home," Bessie said, hanging her head. They walked past a colored man sitting at a desk reading a book. He wore a blue pinstripe suit and a bow tie. His full face sported glasses and a thick mustache. His waved brown hair was parted down the middle.

"Excuse me, children," he said. "Let me introduce myself. I'm Arthur Schomburg."

"Arthur A. Schomburg?" Lillian almost shouted. "I saw

your name over there on that bookcase. My father has
told me about you. You collected a lot of the books in this
library, didn't you?"

"Yes, I did," Mr. Schomburg said.

"I'm sorry, sir, but we need to go," Bessie said, wishing
Lillian would come on.

Mr. Schomburg stood up. "Did I hear you asking
about the Dark Tower?"

Bessie perked up. "Yes, sir, we were," she said. "But it's
a thing and not a place like we thought."

"As a matter of fact, there *is* a place called the Dark
Tower," Mr. Schomburg said.

Bessie's heart began to thump. "Do you know where
it is?" she asked.

"Yes. It's at 108-110 West 136th Street. Here, I'll write
the address down for you."

Bessie's entire body shook as she took the piece of
paper. This man had given her the key to finding Papa.

On their way out, the librarian came out from behind
her desk and stopped them.

"Wait just a minute. I had no idea you were looking
for that place," the librarian said. "It's not for children,
you know. I've heard some pretty wild stories about that
place."

As soon as they were outside, Bessie said, "Let's go to
the Dark Tower right now."

Lillian shook her head. "We have to be home before

supper. We don't have time to look for it. Besides," she said, "didn't you hear the librarian? She said she'd heard wild stories. And it *is* called the *Dark* Tower."

"It c-c-could be scary," Eddie said.

"Or dangerous," Lillian added.

"Then tomorrow I'll go alone," Bessie said, even though she agreed it sounded like a scary place. But if that's where she could find this Miss A'Lelia Walker and Papa, nothing would stop her from going to the Dark Tower.

CHAPTER 7

FIXING LEGS

All the way home, Bessie thought about the Dark Tower. Lillian and Eddie must have been thinking about it, too. Nobody was talking.

Bessie wondered what she could say when she saw Miss A'Lelia Walker. Would she be able to just walk right into the Dark Tower, or would there be an adult outside to keep children out, like at the rent party? Could she go there and ask for Papa? If she did, what would Papa do when he found out she'd been snooping around in grown folks' business? Would he whip her? Bessie didn't care.

But suppose he refused to leave? If that happened, there was nothing she could do. Nothing.

In that moment Bessie understood what action she must take. It was the only way. As they neared their block, Bessie said, "Lillian, do you think Miss Flo can put a conjure on a *woman*?"

"I don't know," Lillian said, stopping. "But what I do know is that going to that Dark Tower doesn't seem like a good idea."

"I-I don't think y-you should g-go, either," Eddie said. "What if it's a really b-bad place?"

They were almost home. "Eddie, you wait on our stoop. If you see Aunt Esther, tell her that Lillian and me went around the corner to the store." Then she took Lillian by the hand and pulled her along.

"W-w-where you g-g-going?" Eddie asked.

"Yes," Lillian said, stopping. "Where *are* we going? I'm not going to that Tower."

"We're going to see Miss Flo," Bessie said.

"Miss Flo?" Lillian said. "Are you crazy?"

"If Miss Flo can put a conjure on a man to make him fall in love, then she can put a conjure on a woman, too. I'm going to ask Miss Flo to put a conjure on Miss Walker."

"I'm not going," Lillian said.

"You have to come with me. You know her better than I do. Please. You said you'd help."

"Are you sure you know what you're doing?" Lillian asked.

Bessie nodded.

"Well, I did say I'd help. All right. I'll go with you," Lillian said. "I'd rather go see Miss Flo than go to that Dark Tower place anyway."

"I-I-I w-w-want to go with you," Eddie said.

"No. It's not safe," Bessie said. "You can help by doing what I asked you, please." She didn't want Eddie to get mixed up in this. Bessie was afraid of what might happen. There was no reason to put Eddie in danger, too.

Eddie stomped on the ground. "It's n-not f-f-fair."

Bessie understood then that being without Mama and Papa must be even harder on Eddie than it was on her. After all, he was younger. Plus, Aunt Esther was always on him about stuttering. But this had to be done, and she couldn't risk getting Eddie hurt. She was his big sister. She had to protect him. Bessie hugged Eddie. "Please," she pleaded.

He shrugged. "But if you're not b-b-back soon, I-I-I'm coming to get you."

Bessie and Lillian walked down to the end of the block and up Miss Flo's steps.

As Bessie reached up to ring the doorbell, she froze. There was white powder all over the top steps. "What is that?" Bessie whispered, pointing.

"It's a part of her conjures," Lillian answered. "Don't step on it. Your feet might fall off!"

"Maybe this is a bad idea," Bessie said. "Maybe I should just go to the Dark Tower and ask Miss Walker for Papa."

"And what will you do if she refuses to let you see

him?" Lillian said. "No, you're right, this is a better idea. Miss Flo must get rid of the woman so your parents can get back together. You don't want to live with your aunts forever, do you?"

Bessie rang the doorbell. Her knees shook. Sweat popped out on her forehead. But she felt better knowing that she didn't have to face Miss Flo alone.

When Miss Flo opened the door, Lillian blurted out, "Good afternoon, Miss Flo. She wants to ask you something," and shoved Bessie forward.

"What can Miss Flo help you with, me dears?" Miss Flo asked.

"Uhh . . . uhh," Bessie stammered. "I want to put a conjure on somebody and I . . ."

"Come in then," Miss Flo said, smiling and motioning them inside. "Come right in."

Bessie stood at the door, so frightened she couldn't open her mouth or move.

"Come in," Miss Flo said again. "If you girls would like help, you must come inside and sit."

"I'm not allowed in anyone's house," Lillian said, looking scared as a rabbit in a trap.

Bessie spun around. "You didn't tell me that you couldn't go in."

"I'll wait out here," Lillian said, backing up and taking a tiny hop to avoid stepping in the white powder.

Miss Flo looked down at the powder. "It all right.

Miss Flo will discuss this matter with Miss Bessie, alone."

Bessie was frozen with terror. It had not occurred to her that she might be left alone in the house with Miss Flo. Tiny beads of sweat trickled down Bessie's forehead and under her arms. But she knew she would have to go inside if she wanted Miss Flo's help.

"You're not going to just stand there now, are you?" Miss Flo said. "Come in and rest your legs."

A vision of the one-legged man popped into Bessie's mind. She reached down and felt her leg.

"Your leg hurting you, child?" Miss Flo asked.

Bessie shook her head. Why did she bring attention to her leg?

Miss Flo eyed Bessie. "I take a look at your leg for you."

Bessie's heart raced. Maybe involving Miss Flo was a bad idea.

"Come on now," Miss Flo said, gripping Bessie's hand and pulling her into the room. She closed the door.

Bessie wanted to run back out and not stop until she reached Burlington. But instead, she stood quiet and still as a possum. The room behind Miss Flo was filled with bright colors. The rug on the floor was orange, navy blue, and red. There were splashes of red all over the room. Miss Flo was barefoot.

"You a smart girl. Come, sit, me child," Miss Flo said, pointing Bessie to a beautiful, squash-colored stuffed chair. "Tell me, what the problem? You look worried as a snake in a mongoose's hut."

Bessie sat down, wringing her hands. What could she say? This woman was a stranger to her. She couldn't tell her about Papa. Bessie felt tears streaming down her face. She wiped them off with the back of her hand. She stood up.

"Please, sit. Miss Flo help you with your burden. You hurting, but, I assure you, things not as they seem."

Bessie cleared her throat. She fingered her Memaw necklace. Bessie knew, even though her mind felt like a jumble of knitting yarn, that she had to get help for her family. She could not wait any longer. It had to be done. "I need to have a conjure put on a woman who is stealing my papa from my mama."

"I see," Miss Flo said. "You coming to Miss Flo for a conjure, now would you? It ain't an easy thing, you know. What you call a conjure is mean business, me little sister. Grown folks' business. No matter the age, truth the same. What you send out always what you get back. But for you, I give a conjure," Miss Flo said, smiling, as she stood up. "Wait here."

Bessie stopped breathing. Did she really want to get a conjure? Yes. Anything to get Papa and Mama back together.

Miss Flo came back with a package wrapped in cloth. "Here, take this. This the thing that you need. Something to take your mind off your worries. That why you come to Miss Flo, right?"

"Don't you need to know the woman's name?" Bessie asked.

"Miss Flo know what you need and the name she needs to know. Now, are you ready?"

Bessie nodded her head. Her hands shook as she held them out to receive the conjure. Then suddenly it occurred to Bessie that they had not talked about how much Miss Flo would charge. Bessie didn't have much money.

She jerked her hands back before touching the conjure. "How much does the conjure cost?"

"No problem, dear girl. Miss Flo happy to see a smile come over that beautiful face. No need for money, you make payment another way. You just promise Miss Flo one thing and that payment enough."

"Yes, ma'am," Bessie said, positive now that she'd do anything to get her parents back together. Whatever she'd have to pay, she'd pay it. And suddenly she knew— she knew what Miss Flo wanted from her in exchange for the conjure. "Yes," Bessie blurted out. "I promise you my leg."

"Your leg?" Miss Flo said, her forehead furrowing. "What this talking 'bout your leg?"

"We—we saw the man. We didn't mean to, but we saw him."

"What man you see?" Miss Flo asked, narrowing her eyes.

"The one whose leg you took," Bessie whispered, as though somehow saying it softly made it less scary.

"Ha!" Miss Flo said, bursting into laughter. "You talking 'bout me Uncle John. You see him leave without his leg, huh? It over there. See?" Miss Flo pointed to a corner.

Bessie didn't want to look, so she shut her eyes. Then she took a deep breath, looked over in the corner, and gasped.

A leg with a sock on it stood in the corner. "That's his leg?" she asked, trembling.

"Yes. His artificial leg. Miss Flo a wood carver, take care of his leg when it don't fit good. Shave it a little," Miss Flo said.

"It's a *wooden* leg?" Bessie felt foolish now. "I'm sorry. We thought that you'd taken that man's leg off."

Miss Flo smiled. "No, Miss Flo won't be needing your leg, but me asking you this favor, for you to always remember: What be done in the dark, always come to the light. That all Miss Flo asking of you—for you to remember this."

Bessie stood still. Her grandma used to say that.

"Now take what you calling a conjure and think 'bout the things you can do to make your heart feel better." Miss Flo held the package out.

Bessie reached out her hands, and Miss Flo put the conjure in them.

"Let no one see this but you," Miss Flo said. "This a perfect conjure for what you needing, me young bird of paradise."

"How do I use it, Miss Flo?" Bessie asked.

"You will know how to use it," Miss Flo assured her. She led Bessie to the door. "Watch your step on the way out. I spilled a sack of flour on me way from the grocer's, and haven't had time to sweep it up. Don't go getting it on you now."

Bessie thanked Miss Flo as she went out the door.

"I see your little friend still waiting for you," Miss Flo said. Lillian stood on the bottom step.

"You the next time, Miss Lillian," Miss Flo said, and closed the door.

"Did you hear that?" Lillian said, her eyes tearing. "She's going to get me!"

"I don't think so. She's not gonna bother you, Lillian. I think maybe we were wrong about Miss Flo."

"What happened?" Lillian asked. "What did you see? Did she threaten you? Was she mean? Tell me!"

Eddie came running down the sidewalk. "What h-happened? Y-y-you all right? L-l-let me see your leg." He bent down to look.

"Eddie," Bessie said, "we were wrong about her taking the man's leg. It was her uncle's wooden leg, and she was just working on it for him. You know, to make it fit better. She's a wood-carver."

"Don't you see?" Lillian said. "She's just telling you that. She probably turned the man's leg into wood."

Bessie hadn't thought of that. But she didn't think Miss Flo would do that.

"Let me see the conjure," Lillian said.

"I can't," Bessie said, sorry that she couldn't share it with Lillian. But it served Lillian right for letting Bessie go in there alone.

"Please," Lillian begged.

"She told me not to, honest. I'm sorry, I just can't," Bessie said.

"Will you show me later, then?" Lillian asked.

"Yes. After I use it. I'd better go home now," Bessie said. "I need to do this right away."

They started walking up the street. "What about the moon?" Lillian asked.

"What *about* the moon?" Bessie said.

"I have never heard of a conjure that you could perform in the daytime," Lillian replied. "Didn't Miss Flo say anything about the full moon? It doesn't happen until Saturday."

Miss Flo hadn't said anything about the night or the moon. But Bessie agreed that it made sense to do something as secret as a conjure at night. Maybe Miss Flo thought Bessie already knew this.

"I'll wait until tonight to do it," Bessie said. "But I can't wait until Saturday. It might be too late. I want my mama and papa back together as soon as possible." They walked up the stoop. "I'll see you tomorrow."

"And you'll show me the conjure then?" Lillian asked again.

"I'll show it to you after it works. Not before. Nothing can get in the way."

Lillian nodded and opened her door. "You're right. I wouldn't want Miss Flo mad at you. She might turn you into a lizard for showing me."

"Yes. And turn you into a lizard for looking," Bessie added, smiling. But she really wished Lillian hadn't said that. She felt a shiver of coldness come over her as she and Eddie walked inside the house.

CHAPTER 8
THE CONJURE

Inside, Aunt Nellie and Aunt Esther were having a heated discussion in the parlor. Bessie wasn't sure what they were arguing about in whispered tones, but she suspected it might be about Papa.

Aunt Esther called to them to get washed up for supper.

"Bessie, can *I* see it?" Eddie asked when they had gone upstairs.

"No. I'm sorry, Eddie. Miss Flo really did tell me not to let anyone see it," Bessie said, sliding the conjure under their bed. "Suppose, because I show you, it doesn't work. You want Mama and Papa to get back together, don't you?"

"Y-yes, I do, Bessie. I won't look," Eddie said. "Bessie, you're the bravest p-p-person I know."

"Thank you, Eddie," Bessie said, hugging him. "I think you're brave, too. Now let's go eat supper before Aunt Esther gets suspicious."

After supper, Bessie and Eddie played a few games of checkers. Eddie won each time because Bessie could not concentrate. Finally, Aunt Esther said it was time for them to go to bed.

Lying in bed, Bessie worried that the conjure might not work. She tried to put the thought from her mind. It had to work.

"B-B-Bessie?" Eddie whispered.

"What, Eddie?"

"What if the c-c-conjure don't work?" Eddie asked sleepily.

"Don't worry. It'll work," Bessie said. "And if it doesn't, I'll go to that Dark Tower and make Miss Walker take me to Papa."

Soon Eddie fell asleep, hugging his framed picture of Mama. But not Bessie. She lay awake thinking about how much she missed the stars in the sky of her old room. And Brownie. And Papa. And she recalled what she missed the most about Mama. She missed Mama combing her hair. Bessie fingered her Memaw necklace.

Finally the house was silent. Everyone was asleep. Bessie got up and removed the conjure from under the bed. She tiptoed into Papa's room so she wouldn't wake Eddie.

She sat on the floor in the dark with only a sliver of light coming from the three-quarter moon. The moon's shadows made the room feel creepy and unnatural. Bessie shivered in the darkness as she looked at the package. It was wrapped securely and tied with a string. Bessie set it on the floor and opened it. A feeling like tiny pinpricks danced on her skin.

Bessie stared at the contents of the package—three fancy fountain pens, an inkwell, and a blank notebook. These were the ingredients for a conjure?

Bessie noticed that there was a note card tucked inside the package. Maybe the instructions for the conjure were written down.

Bessie took a candle from the small table in the corner and lit it with a match. She jumped as the flame sparked to life. Bessie moved closer to the window so the moonlight could lend help. She read the note, frowning.

Dear Miss Bessie,

    Your Auntie Nell and me good girlfriends. She come here when the house over there too full of pain and hurt. Keep safe your heart and remember that <u>life</u> is the magic. Your Auntie say you like Langston Hughes. This for you to write your own poems, for poetry heals the heart.

                        Your friend,
                        Miss Flo

What kind of conjure was this? It was a trick. A dirty trick. Bessie picked up the pens and the inkwell. She flipped through the notebook.

Bessie was very angry. This was no conjure. This wouldn't help her get Papa back. She would have to figure some way to do it by herself. Bessie was alone again. She had been so sure the conjure would work. She could hear in her mind her grandma telling conjure tales from slavery times.

She knew what she would do. She would make her own conjure. Grandma had said that the old African conjurers always used herbs or roots of some kind and mixed them up with all kinds of other stuff.

Bessie sneaked downstairs to the kitchen. The house creaked and moaned in the stillness of the dark. Bessie didn't dare turn on a light or make noise. She stood still until her eyes adjusted to the darkness. She tiptoed to the cabinet and took down the ugliest bowl.

She crushed some garlic in the bowl and dropped in the yolk of an egg. Bessie didn't like eggs, but she knew from Grandma's stories that all conjures needed eggs. She wanted to wash the rest of the egg down the sink, but Aunt Esther was soaking greens in it. Bessie poured the egg white into a small cream pitcher and put it in the icebox. She'd get rid of it later.

Now for the slimy part. There had to be something slimy. If she were home, Bessie could get an earthworm from the ground. She hadn't seen a single worm in Harlem. But she'd seen something worse — something so ugly she wasn't sure she would be able to pick it up.

Bessie swallowed hard. She knew what the slimiest, most disgusting thing in the world was, and she knew exactly where it was in Harlem. She opened the back door quietly and walked down the steps, careful not to spill her mixture.

By the side of the house, Bessie saw what she was looking for—a fat gray slug, its slimy body gleaming in the moonlight.

She didn't want to pick the slug up with her bare hands. But no, this wasn't supposed to be easy. Bessie figured a conjure, if it was to work, required the greatest bravery and sacrifice. Bessie squeezed her eyes shut, took a deep breath, and picked up the slug. A shiver ran up her spine. The slug didn't wiggle at all, but Bessie still felt disgusted and faint. She dropped it in the bowl. Then she yanked out seven strands of her own hair and put them in, too. Grandma always told her seven was a magic number in Africa.

Bessie didn't know what to do next. She found a stick and stirred the conjure up. *You must have to say something magic,* she thought, but she didn't know any magic words. She'd have to make it up.

Bessie knelt down on a small patch of damp grass. She lifted the bowl up to the sky. "Please, God," Bessie said. It seemed strange to pray to God about a conjure, but didn't God make everything? "Let something happen to bring my papa back. Make something bad happen to the woman who took him away from my mama. And let my mama come here with us to Harlem. Amen."

Bessie sat staring at the conjure in the bowl for a short while. A bird chirped. Bessie looked up and realized that dawn was near. She quickly used Aunt Nellie's small planting shovel to dig a hole in the ground. She scraped her conjure into the hole and covered it up. Grandma said everything must return to the earth. Bessie figured the conjure must, too.

In the kitchen, she put the bowl away dirty, because she didn't want to turn the water on and risk waking her aunts. She'd wash it in the morning when she emptied the pitcher out. Now she needed to hurry back to bed before Aunt Esther or Aunt Nellie caught her up.

Once in bed, Bessie could hear Miss Flo's warning: *What be done in the dark, always come to the light.* Maybe she shouldn't have made the conjure. "I hope you're not mad at me, God, for making a conjure," she whispered. "But I do hope it works." Then, exhausted, Bessie fell asleep.

The next morning Aunt Esther called Bessie and Eddie down for breakfast.

"I did the conjure," Bessie whispered to Eddie on the way downstairs. "Don't worry."

Instead of the standard Cream of Wheat, Aunt Esther was stirring a pot of oatmeal at the stove when Bessie and Eddie walked into the kitchen.

"Bessie, go upstairs and get me that sweater on my bed," Aunt Esther said. "It's getting a little chilly 'round here in the mornings."

"Yes, ma'am," Bessie said and went to fetch the sweater. When she returned, Eddie was already at the table, eating his oatmeal.

"I'm making you children a little surprise. I know how fond you are of oatmeal. And I'm going to make a little something to go with it—strawberries and cream," Aunt Esther said. "Maybe that will help you feel better."

Bessie froze. Her oatmeal was in the ugly bowl—the very same bowl that the slug, her hair, and the egg yolk had been in. Bessie gulped. Now she wished she'd washed the bowl out. She thought of Miss Flo's words: *What you send out always what you get back.*

Bessie watched Aunt Esther reach into the icebox and take out the pitcher with the egg white in it. Without looking inside, Aunt Esther poured some cream from a bottle into the pitcher and then dropped some crushed strawberries in it.

"We're all going to have some strawberries and cream," she said brightly.

Bessie felt rooted to the spot.

Aunt Esther sat down at the table and whipped her

napkin onto her lap. "Bessie, sit down. Here." She poured the mixture onto Bessie's oatmeal.

Bessie sat down and stared at the oatmeal with the cream, strawberry, and egg white swimming on top.

Then Aunt Esther said, smiling proudly, "Bessie, that bowl is special. I bet you didn't know it. That bowl belonged to your grandma. I know how much you loved her. I hope it makes you feel closer to home."

When those words spilled from Aunt Esther's mouth, Bessie knew she should not have made the conjure. All signs pointed to the words Miss Flo had asked Bessie to remember: *What be done in the dark, always come to the light.*

Bessie closed her eyes, swallowed hard, and ate what she deserved. She knew now that it was wrong to try to put a conjure on Miss A'Lelia Walker. Deep in her heart, Bessie knew her conjure hadn't worked. The rumors about Miss Flo being a hoodoo woman were not true. They were probably just mean gossip because Miss Flo was different. Like Lillian, she was from another place.

"We'd like to be excused, please," Bessie said when she and Eddie had finished eating.

Aunt Esther cleared her throat. "Well, I suppose . . ." She hesitated. "Oh, all right. You can go."

Just then, Aunt Nellie rushed into the kitchen carrying a folded sheet of paper. "Esther, don't you have something for them?" She passed Aunt Esther the paper.

Aunt Esther gave Aunt Nellie a look. "I suppose it won't upset them too much. Children," she said, clearing her throat again, "I have a note to you from your mama. Sit down and I'll read it to you."

Bessie stared at Eddie. Was it true? Could Mama have written them a letter?

"I can read it," Bessie volunteered.

"Some of it is to us, so why not let Esther read it?" Aunt Nellie said, tugging her ear. "We can see you're worried sick about your parents."

"And didn't I tell you that we don't burden children with grown folks' problems?" Aunt Esther said. "Our own papa said people shouldn't put their worries on the shoulders of children."

"Our own papa," Aunt Nellie said, "didn't want us to know he was a drunk, Esther."

"Hush your mouth," Aunt Esther said loudly.

"Don't tell me to hush," Aunt Nellie continued. "You're always trying to control everything. What are you going to do when you lose the house and we're set out-doors? They'll know something then."

"I cannot believe you are airing out our family linen in front of these children. I want you out of here if you can't abide by my rules. Now hush up."

"I can't take this much longer. I'm going out," Aunt Nellie said and stormed out of the room.

Bessie reached for Eddie's hand. What were they

talking about? Was Aunt Esther going to lose her house?

"Don't pay Baby Sister any mind. She's just not feeling well these days," Aunt Esther said. "Now, I'll read the letter for you children. I'll skip the parts that don't concern y'all. And don't let your parents worry your mind. Just remember, I'm here to take care of you."

Bessie looked at Eddie. He squeezed her hand. Aunt Esther began reading:

Dear children,

We don't want you to worry. We are fine, both Papa and me. Papa is working hard on the docks in New Jersey. Be good. Mind your aunts and stay out of trouble. We hope to see you soon.

I'll write again. And remember what your grandma always told you. Everything will be all right as long as you're with family.

Love,
Mama

When Aunt Esther finished reading, she folded the letter back up and stuck it inside her blouse.

"Aunt Esther, did Mama write that letter herself?" Bessie asked, trembling. "And does that mean Mama knows where Papa is?"

"I can't for the life of me understand why you children ask so many questions," Aunt Esther said. "Now, I've told you what you needed to know—that your mama and papa are all right, no matter where they are. The rest of the letter was not meant for you or Eddie. Now you children run along and play."

"Yes, ma'am," Bessie said.

Eddie nodded his head. He rarely spoke in front of Aunt Esther anymore. They went upstairs to their room.

Bessie was thinking hard on what her aunt had read to them.

"Do you think Mama really wrote that letter?" Bessie asked Eddie. "I don't think she did. Mama can't read and write that well. Remember, she stopped school in third grade. And even if someone wrote it down for her, it didn't sound much like Mama."

"D-d-do you think Aunt Esther would fib?" Eddie asked.

"No, I don't think so. Aunt Nellie will fib to cover up for someone, though. She does it for Papa. Plus, I'm sure I saw that same notepaper on Aunt Nellie's dresser the day she showed us her room."

"D-does that mean that Mama and Papa are n-n-never coming back?" Eddie was beginning to tear up.

"Don't say that, Eddie," Bessie said. "Mama and Papa would never leave us here forever. Even if they're separated, one of them will come back for us. Don't worry." But deep in her heart, Bessie wasn't so sure that things were going to work out.

The conjure plan hadn't worked. There was only one thing left to do, and Bessie needed to do it tomorrow. She would go to the Dark Tower and make Papa come back home.

CHAPTER 9
GETTING THERE

The next day was Saturday. Saturday nights were the only times both Aunt Esther and Aunt Nellie went out. Aunt Esther went to church, and Aunt Nellie always said she had someplace special to go, probably so Aunt Esther wouldn't make her go to church, too. Bessie figured Saturday night was her only chance to sneak away long enough to get to the Dark Tower.

On Saturday morning, Bessie and Eddie met Lillian out on the stoop.

"I'm going to the Dark Tower tonight," Bessie said.

"W-What about me?" Eddie asked.

"You have to go to church with Aunt Esther and make sure she doesn't come home early," Bessie said.

"I still don't think you should go," Lillian said. "The Dark Tower might be some sort of dungeon that people can never leave."

"It c-c-could be an evil p-place," Eddie added.

"It doesn't matter if the devil himself is there. I'm going," Bessie said.

"But how are you going to get in?" Lillian asked. "It's just for grown-ups, remember?"

"I know," Bessie said, remembering being chased away from the rent party. "Wait a minute. I could dress up in Aunt Nellie's clothes and put on makeup! I could just act like I'm a grown-up."

"That might work," Lillian said.

"What about y-your shoes?" Eddie said, pointing to her brown oxfords. They were the only shoes she had.

"I hadn't thought of that," Bessie said. "And Aunt Nellie's high heels are too big for me."

"You could wear my mother's shoes. Her feet are small like yours. I could sneak them out and hide them under that bush over there for you." Lillian pointed to a shrub beside the steps.

"Thanks, Lillian. And I'll wear one of Aunt Nellie's hats to cover my hair."

"It sounds like a good plan," Lillian said. "But how are you going to get away from your auntie?"

Bessie's heart sank. How *was* she going to get away? Aunt Esther always insisted that Bessie and Eddie go with her to church.

"I c-c-could pretend to b-be Lillian's mama," Eddie said excitedly, "and ask Aunt Esther to l-let you visit with

Lil-lil-lian tonight while Aunt Esther g-goes to church."

"That's a good idea, Eddie," Bessie said. "Then I could just act like I was going to Lillian's house. And her parents wouldn't really have to know anything about it."

"Eddie?" Lillian said. "Eddie couldn't pretend to be my mother. It would never work. My mother speaks perfect English. Plus, your aunt could see that it wasn't her."

"What if Eddie—I mean your mother—asked Aunt Esther over the back fence, while she's hanging out the wash this afternoon? Aunt Esther always does the wash on Saturday before she goes to church. I think it might work. Eddie could wear one of your mother's big straw hats and stand up on a box or something so he'd be taller."

"Even if he is behind the fence and she doesn't see him, that is still not going to make Eddie sound like my mother," Lillian said.

"Go on, show her, Eddie," Bessie said.

Eddie cleared his throat. He closed his eyes and then opened them. "Lillian, please come in for dinner," he said, making his voice sound high and sing-songy like Lillian's mother's. He didn't stutter at all. "You have to practice the piano before we eat."

Lillian stared at Eddie. "That is amazing. How can you do that?"

"I-I-I d-d-don't know," Eddie said.

"Eddie can sing without stuttering, too. He has a beautiful voice," Bessie said.

Lillian stared at Eddie and shook her head. "That is incredible."

❧

Bessie stayed in the kitchen after lunch. Her job was to get Aunt Esther into the backyard at the right time.

"Aunt Esther, would you like me to help you hang out the clothes?" Bessie asked. "I always used to help Mama."

"Lord, I thought you children didn't like doing your chores," Aunt Esther said, eyeing Bessie suspiciously.

"No, ma'am. We just never had so many nice things to dust and clean like yours, Aunt Esther. We're afraid we'll break your things. Like the vase," Bessie said.

"What vase?" Aunt Esther said. "What vase did you break?"

Bessie's throat tightened. Why had she said that? "The vase that was in the hall. Eddie broke it accidentally," she said, realizing it wouldn't help to fib now.

"Oh. Now I see. Your papa told me he broke the vase. You children," Aunt Esther said with a sigh. "You know, when your papa was a little boy, he was the clumsiest thing. I suppose your little brother is just like him, then?"

Bessie nodded her head.

"I always had to look out after them two, Little Ed and Baby Sister, back in North Carolina when we was growing up. Yep, just like they was my own. I ain't never had much childhood," Aunt Esther said, looking off into space.

"I'm sorry," Bessie said.

"Sorry? Sorry for what?" Aunt Esther asked.

"Grandma used to tell me that she always hated you ain't had much of a childhood," Bessie said. "That's why she liked to see me and Eddie playing a lot. She never wanted us to do many heavy chores on account of it."

"Are you saying that my mama knew I missed my childhood?" Aunt Esther said.

"Yes, ma'am," Bessie said. "Grandma always said that's why she forgave you for not coming to see her much. She said you had a right to be mad at her for making you grow up so fast."

Aunt Esther plopped down on a chair. She wiped her eyes with her apron.

Bessie could see she was crying. Now Bessie understood Aunt Esther better. Maybe Aunt Esther didn't want to tell them anything or worry them about Mama and Papa so *they* wouldn't miss *their* childhood. Maybe she did mean them well. Now Bessie felt bad about fooling Aunt Esther. But she had to find out where Papa was, and she didn't think Aunt Esther would tell her, even now.

Bessie heard a whippoorwill's shrill whistle coming through the window.

"Lord, is that a whippoorwill I hear?" Aunt Esther said. "No, it can't be. Ain't no whippoorwills in Harlem.

Plus, they don't come out in the daytime. I must be hearing things." Bessie flinched. She'd forgotten that whippoorwills only sing at night.

Aunt Esther dried her eyes and picked up her laundry basket.

"May I help you, Aunt Esther?" Bessie asked again. Then she noticed that the basket was full of white clothes, and she worried that Aunt Esther might say no. Even Mama didn't let Bessie help with the whites because she thought Bessie might get them dirty while hanging them on the line.

"You can help if you want," Aunt Esther said. "Come on, then."

Outside, Bessie said quickly, "I'll hold the clothespins for you. Let's start over here." Bessie moved over close to the fence that separated Aunt Esther's yard from Lillian's yard. She knew Eddie was already in place. He was the Harlem whippoorwill. She handed Aunt Esther a clothespin and cleared her throat loudly.

"Good afternoon, Mrs. Henry. How do you do this fine Saturday?" said the voice on the other side of the fence.

"I'm fine, Mrs. Moore. I do fine. And your family?" Aunt Esther said, craning her neck to see over the fence.

"My family is peachy fine," the voice said.

Bessie grimaced. *Peachy fine?*

"I'm glad you're outside," the voice continued. "I

wanted to ask your permission for Miss Bessie to spend some time with my Lillian this evening."

"I'm sorry, but I have to go to church, Mrs. Moore," Aunt Esther said, bending to pick up a shirt. "It's the beginning of revival at our church, and I wouldn't be able to fetch Bessie until after ten o'clock."

"That would be perfectly fine," the voice said. "We would be delighted to have Miss Bessie's company."

"If you're sure she won't be any trouble?" Aunt Esther said, sounding her most proper.

"No trouble at all. She's no trouble. She and that fine young man Eddie are two smart children."

"Yes, they are both very smart," Aunt Esther said.

Then, to Bessie's horror, she heard a giggle.

"Are you all right, Mrs. Moore?" Aunt Esther asked, rising up on her tiptoes to see over the fence.

Bessie jumped in front of Aunt Esther. "There's something crawling on your face, Aunt Esther! Let me get it off," she said loudly.

"What?" Aunt Esther said, slapping at her face. "What in the world is it, child? Where? Where?"

"Here, I'll get it for you, Aunt Esther," Bessie said, reaching up and pretending to grab something. "Oops, it flew away."

Aunt Esther walked to the fence and peered over. "Excuse me, Mrs. Moore," she said. "Mrs. Moore? Mrs. Moore?"

"I think she went back inside, Aunt Esther," Bessie said, sighing with relief.

"You know, Bessie," Aunt Esther said, "that woman has the most elegant speech. Lord knows, I wish your brother could speak that well."

"Me too, Aunt Esther," Bessie said. "I think one day Eddie will speak that well. I truly believe so."

After finishing the laundry with Aunt Esther, Bessie walked around to the front of the house. Eddie sat on the stoop.

"You did a good job, Eddie," Bessie said. Then she noticed their neighbors' furniture outside on the curb. The Wades lived next door to Aunt Esther. They were a quiet elderly couple who knew Aunt Esther and sometimes came over to sit with her in the evenings.

Bessie rushed into the sitting room, where her two aunts were arguing. Eddie followed her into the room. "Aunt Esther, are the Wades moving?" Bessie asked.

"You're supposed to say 'excuse me' when you interrupt grown folks, Bessie," Aunt Esther said. "And boy, fix your shirt," she added, glaring at Eddie.

"Excuse me, Aunt Esther," Bessie said, "but are the Wades moving?"

While Eddie struggled to tuck his shirttail into his

pants, Aunt Nellie blurted out, "They've been set out for not paying their rent."

"You shouldn't be syndicating in grown folks' business, Bessie Carol Coulter," Aunt Esther said. Then she turned back to Aunt Nellie. "What is wrong with you, Baby Sister, speaking out of turn in front of these children like that? We don't tell children in this family that sort of business, and you know it. Now, be quiet."

Bessie could not believe what happened next. Aunt Nellie exploded like a shot from a gun.

"No, we don't tell them nothing. We let them worry themselves to death about what's happening to their parents. We don't tell them that if we don't find some money soon, we are gonna all be outdoors, because we're paying thirty dollars a month for a house that would cost ten dollars if we weren't colored."

"Nellie!" Aunt Esther said, "don't burden the children. Now hush."

"I won't keep quiet any longer," Aunt Nellie said. "If I'd kept my job at Small's Paradise, we would have money. But you were the one who wanted me to quit, saying it wasn't fit for a Christian woman. Now look at us. Ed's run off, and we can't afford to stay here unless I get a job doing what you don't approve of me doing."

Eddie's head shot up and he stopped fidgeting with his suspenders. Bessie gasped. Aunt Nellie's words ran around and around in her head. *Ed's run off.* She couldn't hold it in any longer. "Where is Papa run off to?" she interrupted.

Aunt Esther shook her head. "See what you've done, Baby Sister? Now you've gone and worried the children."

"Bessie, I told you and Eddie your papa is away working," Nellie said, stooping down in front of them, tugging her ear furiously. "That's all I meant. We don't want y'all worried, but—"

"If you say one more word," Aunt Esther said, her teeth clenched, "I will put you out on the street right now, Nellie Coulter Johnson. And you're correct, I will not have you flouncing around dancing."

"Do you know what?" Aunt Nellie said, rising up. "I'm a grown woman. And I don't mean you no disrespect, but you're my sister, not my mama. I'm gonna start dancing again because that's what I love. And if you can't accept that, I will move out."

Aunt Esther walked to a chair and collapsed in it. She sat there holding her head and sobbing softly, as though she were all alone in the room.

"I'm sorry," Aunt Nellie said. "I do love you. But you can't run everything, Esther. And you can't be responsible for everyone, either." Aunt Nellie glanced at the clock. "I'm late. I've got someplace to go tonight." And she rushed from the room.

Bessie and Eddie watched Aunt Esther. Bessie didn't know what to say to make Aunt Esther stop crying.

Finally, Eddie went over to Aunt Esther. He took the handkerchief from her pocket and began to wipe Aunt Esther's tears. He started to softly sing the hymn, "His Eye Is on the Sparrow."

Bessie loved this song, so she sat down and listened while she thought of Papa and Mama and how things used to be back home. She could see Mama and Papa and her and Eddie sitting close together at church—Bessie leaning on Papa, and Eddie leaning on her, singing.

When Eddie was finished, Aunt Esther stopped and looked up. "Sweet Jesus, you have the most beautiful voice I have ever heard." Aunt Esther grabbed Eddie. "Lord, boy, come here and give me a hug. You have touched my very soul."

After supper Aunt Esther got ready for church. She was still talking about being amazed that Eddie didn't stutter while singing as she and Eddie headed toward the front door.

Eddie hung back and whispered to Bessie, "What if you're not b-back when m-me and Aunt Esther get back? Sh-she said she'd be b-b-back at ten."

"I don't know. I'll try to be back," Bessie said.

"Behave yourself at the Moores', Bessie," Aunt Esther said as she pulled on her gloves. She took Eddie by the hand. Bessie couldn't help but smile. She decided Eddie's singing could melt ice on a frozen pond.

As soon as Aunt Esther and Eddie left, Bessie went into Aunt Nellie's room. She would apologize to Aunt Nellie later for going into her bedroom without permission. It didn't take Bessie long to put on Aunt Nellie's makeup from her dresser. She stopped for only a second to examine the notepaper on the dresser. She was right—this was the same paper that the letter from Mama was written on.

Downstairs in the sewing room, Bessie opened Aunt Nellie's trunk. She put on stockings and a shimmery scarlet dress with a ruffle at the top and a long, low waist. Bessie straightened the sash and smoothed out the big bow that was attached on the front. The dress hung on her like a sack.

Bessie took her hair out of the plaits. She combed it and pinned it up. Now she looked more grownup. Then she put on one of Aunt Nellie's flop hats.

Outside, Bessie checked under the bush. Lillian had not chickened out. Wrapped in paper were Lillian's mother's high-heeled shoes, better known as "spikes." They were shiny gold. When Bessie slipped them on, she thought of Cinderella.

Bessie wobbled around for a while, trying to keep her balance. *How in the world do women walk in these shoes?* she wondered. She teetered down the street in the direction of the Dark Tower, following the street signs and checking the map Lillian had lent her.

The bottoms of Bessie's feet burned by the time she'd reached the corner of 124th Street. She stumbled and fell, lost a shoe, stuck it back on, and weaved some more as she made her way toward the Dark Tower. She looked in the windows of Loft's Candy Shop for only a second and continued walking as fast as she could.

On Lenox Avenue, almost everyone was dressed up. Men wore striped silk shirtsleeves and tan shoes with squared-off bulldog toes. A few women still had on uniforms and thick-soled shoes from day work. But many more wore bright gingham and low-scooped dresses. Others were dressed in silks and chiffons, with huge flowered hats on their heads and beaded purses over their arms.

Down the block, the words *Lafayette* and *Vaudeville* were lit up on signs. A crowd of people mingled outside the Lafayette Theater. The marquee advertised Bessie Smith in a musical revue called *Mississippi Days.*

Bessie spied a clock through a storefront window as she walked by. It was seven o'clock already. She needed to hurry. She pulled off her shoes and carried them in her hands. Now people stared as she whizzed by them, her shoes swinging in her hands.

The farther Bessie walked, the fancier the people were dressed. Finally, she was near Jungle Alley. Once when

they were "airing out," Aunt Nellie had told Bessie that
the part of Harlem called Jungle Alley was nothing but
cabarets and nightclubs. She said it was a "hot spot—no
children allowed." Bessie was glad she didn't have to pass
through Jungle Alley.

Just as she passed a place called Tillie's Chicken Shack,
an old man whipped his hand out quicker than a frog
catching flies. He caught Bessie by the arm. "Where you
going in such a speedy hurry, girl?"

Bessie pulled away, frightened. "Please, turn me loose,"
she said. She could see that the man was drunk.

"You a pretty thing," the man said, not letting go of
Bessie's arm. She tried to jerk away, but he grabbed her
and pulled her toward him. Bessie spun around and kicked
him. Then she ran.

The old man stumbled after her. Bessie's heart pounded
furiously. Would he hurt her? She frantically looked around
to see if anyone was paying attention. People seemed not
to notice the commotion. Bessie realized that they thought
she was a grown woman and could take care of herself.

Bessie reached a corner. She looked around and spotted
a broken cobblestone. She picked it up, turned, and took
aim. *Bang.* The rock smashed into a doorpost just as the
man passed by it.

It took him a moment to realize Bessie had thrown it.
"Go on. Git!" he yelled at her. "I don't want to be bothered
with you anyhow."

Bessie ran and didn't slow down until she realized she had run right into Jungle Alley. She was tired and out of breath. Her stomach flipped over and over. Should she go back home? This was dangerous.

But she couldn't. She was going to the Dark Tower. Bessie took a deep breath and began walking briskly. Her only thoughts were about Papa. She must make Papa come back. Then she must make Papa go see about Mama and fix everything. There was nothing else to do.

CHAPTER 10

THE DARKEST HOUR

Bessie hurried through Jungle Alley. Lights flashed, car horns blared, and words blinked on marquees along the street. Bessie's legs were tired, her feet swollen and cut, and she wanted to go back home. She slowed down near Small's Paradise, where Aunt Nellie used to work.

Bessie was staring up at the building, giving herself a breather, when she recognized a voice—Aunt Nellie! She was coming down the street, talking loudly to a man. "Yes, I *do* want my job back," Bessie could hear her saying.

Bessie quickly moved closer to the shadowy entrance of a building. She lowered her head and pulled down the flop hat. Bessie couldn't run now or Aunt Nellie would notice her. She shifted on her legs and held her breath.

They passed so close that Bessie could smell the jasmine perfume Aunt Nellie was wearing. Luckily, Aunt Nellie was so busy talking, she didn't notice anyone. The minute Bessie saw them go inside a door, she ran.

She slowed to a snail's pace when she rounded the corner onto 136th Street. She was nearing the Dark Tower. Her chest seared with pain. She limped on her sore feet, panting. Bessie admitted to herself now that she feared the Dark Tower more than anything in her life. The image she had of it was something dark and ugly, like the no-headed man Papa told her about on spooky nights. But she could not afford to let fear stop her. She had to save her family. Nothing was going to stop her from finding Papa.

Heart pounding, Bessie counted the numbers on the huge building fronts. But once she stood across from number 108, she was confused. This *couldn't* be the Dark Tower. Bessie checked the numbers on nearby buildings again. No, this had to be the right place. The building was tall, with three floors of windows. But it wasn't dark or ugly. *Maybe the dark ugliness is on the inside,* Bessie thought. *Maybe it snatches you up the minute you come through the door.*

Bessie walked slowly toward the Dark Tower, counting her steps as she got closer and closer. At the door she spotted a big knocker shaped like the head of a fierce lion. Bessie shivered. Suppose they wouldn't let her in? She looked down at her legs. Her stockings looked terrible. Bessie slipped the shoes onto her swollen feet.

She took a deep breath and readied her hand to bang the knocker. She touched it and squeezed her eyes shut.

Then she heard laughter behind her. She saw a large group of people crossing the street together, laughing and talking loudly. They were all so busy kidding around that Bessie was sure they hadn't seen her. She ran and hid behind the front fender of one of the fancy cars parked along the curb.

She watched one of the men in the crowd bang the lion hard when they reached the door. In a few seconds, a tall colored man wearing a maroon uniform and a white wig opened the door.

Bessie waited for the right moment. When all the people were busy walking in and handing their hats and furs to an attendant, Bessie darted from her hiding place and slipped in among the crowd of people.

Her heart pounded as she passed through the doorway of the Dark Tower. She knew she had only a moment to decide which way to go. Her eyes darted past the entryway. To her right was a large room packed with people laughing and talking. The curving stairway to her left was her only escape. Bessie scooted up the stairs.

At the landing she turned down a long, shadowy hallway. She slipped into the first door she came to. It was a small closet. She knelt down and shut the door quietly, listening to hear if anyone had followed her up the stairs. She heard laughter and loud music blasting from downstairs. Bessie put her ear to the door. She didn't hear any sounds directly outside.

Bessie cracked open the door and looked out. She didn't see anyone. Cautiously she stepped out. The thick rug running down the hallway made her feel like she was walking on a bed. Bessie knew she wouldn't make much noise walking on it.

She moved down the hall, looking behind her every few seconds. She tried the glass knob of the first door she passed. It was locked. As she walked along, jiggling each doorknob, she discovered that every door was locked except the last one. It opened easily, and Bessie slipped inside, shutting the door behind her. The lights were on. Bessie felt swallowed up in the immense, beautiful room.

A large desk with spindly curved legs sat in the center of the room. A statue of a woman sat atop another carved piece of furniture. Arranged around the room were chairs covered in blue velvet and decorated with carvings of lions and other figures. Some of the vases in the room were as tall as Bessie. She walked over to a black piano in one corner. Its gold trim and ivory keys gleamed in the lamplight. The piano's top was open, and Bessie peeped inside.

Bessie warned herself that she should be looking for Papa and not gawking at all the beautiful things. Somewhere in this room might be a clue to Papa's whereabouts. She hurried over to the desk. She opened one drawer and then another. In the middle drawer she found a gold key ring with two long, skinny keys on it. Maybe those keys would unlock some of the other doors. One of the rooms might even be Papa's!

Bessie grabbed the keys and turned toward the door. Then she took a deep breath and stopped. She couldn't believe her eyes. Painted on the wall by the door was the poem "The Weary Blues." She stood still, mesmerized by the words. Then she heard the thud of a door closing down the hall. She'd better find Papa quick, before someone found her.

She slipped into the hallway and hurriedly tried the keys in one locked door after another. None of the doors opened. Then Bessie heard voices coming up the steps. Her hands shook as she tried the keys in another lock. The lock didn't turn. She quickly went to the next door. Still nothing. Bessie looked toward the stairs. The voices were closer, almost at the landing. What could she do? She didn't have time to get back down the long hallway to the unlocked room. She stuck the key in the next door. She closed her eyes and prayed that it would work. The key turned the lock. She ducked into the room and shut the door.

She rested against the door, trying to calm her pounding heart. She listened, praying that whoever was coming up the stairs wasn't headed for this room. Finally, she took a deep breath and turned around to see where she was. A crystal chandelier lit the room. A huge,

cloth-covered object sat on a table in the center of the
room. By the window stood an A-shaped wooden structure. A large white board leaned against its top half, held
in place by a wooden trough that ran across the middle of
the structure. Paints in little tubes and tins were on a
table next to it.

Then Bessie spotted something familiar on a desk. It
looked like one of Papa's old work shirts. She walked over
and picked it up. She smelled it. It was definitely Papa's.
She could smell his spicy scent. Bessie examined the shirt.
It was speckled with many different colors, just like the
shirts in his suitcase.

Next to the desk sat a black satchel that looked like
the one Lillian had described. With shaking fingers, Bessie
unbuckled the satchel and looked inside. It was filled with
tubes of paint and more brushes—the same little paint
tins and brushes with gold bands on them that the man at
the rent party had given Papa. Papa's secret. Papa was
here. In the Dark Tower. Now all Bessie had to do was
find him and make him see that he needed to come back
home with her.

Just then a man's voice boomed right outside the door.
Bessie froze. She saw the doorknob turn and heard the
voice say, "I'll bring it down now."

Bessie needed to hide. But where? There was a cot
against the far wall, but the bed linens were missing. Bessie
ran for the table in the center of the room that held the

tall covered object. She scurried under the tablecloth. She squatted down and tried to stop her heart from beating so fast. Her chest hurt and her throat burned. Her legs ached terribly as she crouched there waiting.

She heard the man open the door and walk into the room. Then she realized he was removing whatever was on top of the table. And he was taking the tablecloth with it. Bessie held her breath. She could not make a sound or the man might look under the table.

With the tablecloth gone, Bessie could see the man. He was a colored man dressed very nicely in a dark blue suit, but he didn't have on any socks with his shoes. Bessie watched him struggle to carry the covered object to the door.

Near the door, he set the bundle down and leaned it against the wall. He reached along the wall and switched off the lights. Then he picked up the big bundle again and walked out, shutting the door behind him.

Bessie crawled out from under the table and dusted herself off. She had to find Papa. She took a step and heard a crunching sound. She had stepped on something. She bent down to pick it up. It was an expensive-looking watch, and she had broken the glass top.

Suddenly the light came back on. A tall, well-dressed white man stood in the doorway. "Who have we here?" he said.

Bessie felt as though she were choking.

"What are you doing here?" he asked. "Does A'Lelia know you're in here? What's that in your hand?"

Bessie wanted to cry.

"Let me see that," he said, taking the watch from Bessie. "Where did you get this, little girl?"

"I-I-I found it," Bessie stammered. *What if he thinks I stole it?* Bessie thought. What if Papa finds out? He would be so ashamed of her. But she didn't steal it. And Papa should be ashamed of *himself*—not Bessie.

"Come with me," the man said, pulling Bessie by the hand.

"Please. I found it," Bessie pleaded, as the man pulled her along. "That man with no socks on, he must have dropped it."

The man took her down the hallway and into the room with the poem on the wall. He called out the door to someone, "Ask A'Lelia to come up here, please."

Bessie fingered her Memaw necklace. It would protect her from evil.

The man turned back to Bessie. "Have a seat. She'll be here in a minute."

Bessie didn't want to sit, but her feet hurt from the shoes and her knees were weak. She sat down on the edge of a velvet chair, waiting. What would A'Lelia Walker do to her? Suppose this woman *was* the devil? Would she throw Bessie out without even letting her see Papa? Would she get Papa and say his thieving daughter was here? Would

she call the police? Or would she do something even more
horrible to Bessie?

Bessie saw the door opening slowly. She squeezed
her eyes shut. She prayed that it was Papa and not Miss
Walker. She opened her eyes slowly. But her prayer was
not answered. A tall woman strode into the room. She
walked over to Bessie and stood directly in front of her.

Miss Walker wore a gold dress with diamonds on it. A
fancy gold turban was wrapped around her jet-black hair.
Her earrings sparkled in the light. Bessie had never seen
a woman so tall or so—she hated to think it, but it was
true—beautiful. She didn't look like a devil, she looked
like a queen.

Bessie cast her eyes down as the man explained where
he'd found Bessie and with what. "Go get Richard Bruce,"
Miss Walker said to the man. He left the room.

Bessie couldn't take it any longer. No matter how
scared she was, she had come to the Dark Tower to get
Papa. And no matter what, even if everyone believed that
she stole the watch, she wasn't leaving without Papa. "I
came to get my papa," Bessie said loudly.

"What?" Miss Walker said. "You came for your papa?"

"Yes. I know he's here. And I want him to come
home to be with us. His family. His children," Bessie
said, feeling braver. No one was going to keep her from
Papa.

Bessie stood up. Her fingers clutched her Memaw

necklace. "I found the watch on the floor. I didn't steal it. I never steal."

"All right, but what were you doing sneaking around in my house?"

"I told you," Bessie said. "I came to get my papa. My mama isn't here in Harlem, so *I* have to get him from you."

"From me?" Miss Walker said. "Who in the world is your papa, child?"

"You know who he is," Bessie said defiantly. "I saw my papa's shirt in that room down the hall. I found those same paint tins and brushes at home in his suitcase. I read the note you wrote him."

"The note?" Then Miss Walker laughed. To Bessie's ears it was a loud and cruel laugh. The laugh of a witch.

"Lord, I know who you are now," Miss Walker said. "You're Ed Coulter's little daughter, Bessie. But why are you dressed like this?"

"I want my papa," Bessie said, balling up her fists at her sides. Bessie was furious that the woman knew her name. Did Papa tell Miss Walker about her and Eddie?

"Your papa was here. You're right about that," Miss Walker said. "But he's gone."

"I don't believe you. He's here, and I want him to come home with us."

"He *is* home," Miss Walker said.

Bessie wished she had a rock. She'd knock this woman over. "This is not Papa's home. His home is with us. With

Mama." Bessie was shaking so hard she could feel her knees hitting together.

"Calm down, honey," Miss Walker said. "I meant that I put him on the train myself, yesterday. He is home — with your mama."

"You're fibbing. I'm not leaving here without Papa," Bessie said. She refused to let this evil woman trick her.

The tall white man walked back into the room. The colored man with no socks on walked in, too. "Hey," the colored man said, smiling at Bessie. "I hear you found my watch. Thank you."

"I'm sorry, sir. I accidentally stepped on it," Bessie said, hoping the man wouldn't be mad.

"It's all right," he said. "Carl here tells me you were hiding in the room."

The white man glanced at Bessie. "Is she all right, A'Lelia?"

"She's looking for Ed," Miss Walker said. "Bessie, meet Richard Bruce Nugent, a writer and artist. And Carl Van Vechten, a novelist and art collector."

"And Miss Bessie's claim to fame?" Mr. Nugent asked.

"Meet Ed Coulter's daughter."

"Did she come for the presentation?" Mr. Van Vechten asked.

Mr. Nugent interrupted. "Splendid. What a fitting tribute. You're a genius, A'Lelia."

"It's not my doing," Miss Walker replied. "Bessie

thought this up all on her own. Didn't you, sweetie?"

Bessie felt more confused and angry than ever. Why weren't they getting her papa for her? Did this woman think she could just break up Bessie's family? She spoke up again. "I only came to get my papa."

"Then you shall have him," Miss Walker said. "Come along with us."

Bessie reluctantly followed her down the stairs. She didn't want to obey this woman, but what else could she do? Maybe when Papa saw her he would feel so bad that Miss Walker's spell would be broken. Bessie held on to the gold-and-black banister so she wouldn't fall in her shoes. When she reached the bottom of the stairs, Bessie looked across the foyer into the grand party room she'd seen before. The crowd of people had gathered in a circle around the huge covered object Mr. Nugent had wrestled downstairs.

Miss Walker grabbed Bessie's hand and pulled her across the foyer and into the center of the room. Bessie couldn't imagine why she was there, unless Miss Walker was going to tell everyone how she'd been sneaking around in her house. Bessie wanted to cry. She held her Memaw necklace tightly for protection and scanned the audience, searching the faces for Papa. But she didn't see him.

All she saw was a glittering crowd of strangers. Women in fancy maids' uniforms walked through the crowd asking, "May I refill your champagne glass for the toast?"

Bessie could see that this room was as beautiful as the one upstairs. A huge bookcase stood against one wall. Fancy red chairs sat beside tables draped with white lace. Flowers sat in the center of each table. An orchestra played in the back of the room.

A'Lelia Walker tapped on a tall, thin glass. "Everyone. As you know, you're here tonight for the unveiling of a painting that Carl Van Vechten and I commissioned of a Negro Madonna and Child. The artist who painted it is a very special man, and we've decided to award the balance of the money due him, a three-thousand-dollar check, tonight."

People in the audience clapped loudly.

Bessie's eyes blurred with embarrassment. Why was she being forced to stand up here?

"Do you see this young woman here?" Miss Walker asked, laying her hand on Bessie's shoulder.

Bessie wanted to die.

A'Lelia Walker continued. "She was daring enough to sneak into the Dark Tower tonight to find out if her father was here. Her father is Ed Coulter."

The audience clapped wildly.

Bessie didn't understand what was happening. She looked from Miss Walker to the Van Vechten man, but they both were grinning, clapping, and looking at her.

"We can agree there are no coincidences, right?" Miss Walker continued. "So, I present to you Ed Coulter's Madonna and Child."

There was a drumroll from the band as Mr. Nugent pulled the cloth off the object. It was a large painting.

Thunderous applause filled the room. Miss Walker held up her hand for the crowd to quiet down.

"Do you recognize anyone in this painting?" she asked. Bessie heard gasps and murmurs from the crowd.

"Bessie," Miss Walker said, pulling her around in front of the painting. "Do *you* recognize anyone in this painting?"

It was Bessie's mama. And she was holding a baby that looked like Bessie. It was just like the drawing Papa had given her of Mama holding her when she was a baby. But the face of the baby in this painting was just like Bessie's face now. Bessie's heart was breaking. Papa painted this beautiful picture of Mama for another woman? It didn't make any sense. Bessie was so confused she couldn't think.

"So now," A'Lelia Walker said, "I'd like to present the check for three thousand dollars to Bessie Carol Coulter, on behalf of her father, who couldn't be here because he wanted to go see about his wife."

Bessie's eyes grew large. What did she mean—see about his wife? Mama?

"Mrs. Coulter has been sick," Miss Walker continued. "She stayed back in North Carolina, where she was being cared for. But Ed Coulter wanted to nurse his wife back to health himself. For weeks, Ed worked on this painting to raise the money to go back to North Carolina. Finally he came here to stay at the Dark Tower so he could finish it as quickly as possible and get back home to his wife." Miss Walker paused, then smiled. "Now that's how a man *ought* to love a woman."

Bessie heard her, but the words were overwhelming. Papa *did* love Mama! He had been here working, just as he said. And now he was back home with Mama.

Bessie heard Miss Walker through her confusion and tears. "And as you can see, folks, he's also raised a brave little girl." The crowd burst into applause as Miss Walker handed Bessie the check.

CHAPTER 11

FAMILY

Afterward Bessie sat and talked to Miss A'Lelia Walker, or Miss A'Lelia, as they agreed Bessie should call her. She introduced Bessie to all the artists, writers, and musicians at the party. Bessie was fascinated that Miss A'Lelia actually knew all these people, including the poet Bessie loved, Langston Hughes. When Miss A'Lelia's driver took Bessie home, she was too excited to care that the lights in the front room were on. Aunt Esther had beat her home.

Aunt Esther opened the door. Bessie hugged her quickly.

"Where on earth have you been?" Aunt Esther burst out. "I have been worried sick."

"So have I," Aunt Nellie said.

"I-I-I'm sorry, Bessie," Eddie said. "I-I tried to m-m-make up something."

"It's all right, Eddie," Bessie said, hugging him.

"And what in the name of heaven do you have on?" Aunt Esther asked.

Before Bessie could answer, Aunt Nellie said, "Wait a minute. Didn't I—? No, that couldn't have been you."

"It was me," Bessie admitted. "But I've got good news. Here, Aunt Esther," Bessie said, handing her aunt the check.

"What is this?" Aunt Esther said. Then she looked at it. "Oh, my goodness. Where did you get this?"

"It belongs to Papa. He worked for it by painting a picture," Bessie said, grinning with pride.

"What are you talking about, Bessie?" Aunt Esther said. "Your papa is in New Jersey working on the docks. Isn't he, Nellie?"

Aunt Nellie was staring down. "No," she said. "He was working, but not in New Jersey. He didn't tell you, Esther, because he knows you disapprove of him painting. Remember how you used to say that a decent family man would find a real job instead of wasting time?"

"What about the letter from Martha?" Aunt Esther asked. "The one written to us and the children saying he was all right and working in New Jersey?"

"I wrote the letter," Aunt Nellie said.

"I knew Mama didn't write it," Bessie said. "And I knew Papa wasn't working in New Jersey on the docks building anything. He left his brogans. Papa never works without them."

"Wait a minute. *You* knew where he was, too?" Aunt Esther asked Bessie. "Where was he?"

"He was staying at the Dark Tower," Bessie said. "He got a job painting a picture of a colored—I mean Negro— Madonna and Child for Miss A'Lelia Walker and a man named Carl Van Vechten."

Aunt Esther's hands flew up to her mouth. "You mean Madame C. J. Walker's daughter?"

"Who is M-Madame Walker?" Eddie asked.

"Why, she's a colored millionaire. She's passed on now, but she was a good, generous woman," Aunt Esther said. "She made her fortune selling things for colored women's hair and skin. Lord have mercy. My brother painting for Madame's daughter!"

"And you met Mr. Carl Van Vechten?" Aunt Nellie asked.

"Yes, he's a very nice man," Bessie said.

"Who's Van-Van—you know?"

"He writes novels about colored people," Aunt Nellie said. "Word is, he helped lots of colored writers meet the big New York publishers, and he collects colored artists' work."

"And my little niece met all those people tonight?" Aunt Esther asked.

"Yes, ma'am," Bessie said. "I went to the Dark Tower for Papa, and that's when I found out the truth."

Bessie told them the whole story. But she left out the

part about Miss Flo. Aunt Esther would never understand that.

"I can't believe it. You children did this all by your-
selves?" Aunt Esther said. She turned to Aunt Nellie.
"And you didn't know about them doing this, either?"

"No, but I'm impressed," Aunt Nellie said, smiling at
Bessie and Eddie.

Bessie smiled back, but then she looked down at the
floor. Miss A'Lelia had given her some serious news, too,
and now it was time to talk about it. Bessie looked at
her aunts.

"Miss A'Lelia told me that Mama has tuberculosis,"
Bessie said.

"What's that?" Eddie asked.

"It's a disease of the lungs," Aunt Nellie said gently.
"Your papa brought you here so you wouldn't catch it
from your mama."

"Miss A'Lelia said no one told us because people are
all ashamed of it," Bessie explained. "Sometimes when
people know that someone in your family has it, they
don't want anything to do with you. Miss A'Lelia said
that's why Mama made Papa promise not to tell us or let
us find out. She was afraid we might tell people and they
would treat us bad, Eddie."

"What about Papa?" Eddie asked. "Is h-he all right,
Bessie?"

"Yes, he is. He's fine. But Miss A'Lelia told me that

right after we got to Harlem, Papa thought he was getting sick, the same as Mama. He didn't want to risk making us sick too, so he wasn't coming home much. I guess that's why he quit saying good night to us, Eddie. But Miss A'Lelia had her doctor check him, and he just had a bad cold. Then we didn't see him because he stayed at the Dark Tower to finish the painting. And now, Papa is with Mama."

Bessie went over and put her arms around her little brother. "Tuberculosis is a terrible disease, Eddie, but it looks like Mama's gonna get well. And Papa's bringing Mama up here to New York as soon as she's strong enough to travel."

"Lord have mercy," Aunt Esther said.

"I didn't even know that part," Aunt Nellie said. "I'm so happy for y'all."

Bessie smiled. "All along, I thought Miss A'Lelia was such a terrible woman. But she's not—she's very nice. She even said Eddie and I could stay with her at her mansion until Mama and Papa get to Harlem."

Aunt Esther looked sad for the first time since Bessie had hugged her. "Well, of course you children would rather go stay in a mansion. I'll miss you," she said gruffly, handing the check back to Bessie. Then she headed toward the kitchen.

"Wait, Aunt Esther," Bessie said. "I have something else to say."

Aunt Esther walked back. "So do I," she said slowly. "It seems I was wrong. You and your brother are old enough to know what is happening to your own family. And me, I'm just an old-fashioned fool. I've been under a heap of strain. I hope you'll forgive me. And you too, Nellie."

"Oh, my goodness," Aunt Nellie said. "You didn't call me 'Baby Sister'? I'm gonna pass right out." Aunt Nellie pretended to faint.

"I have to accept that you're grown, Nellie," Aunt Esther said. "And I want you to stay here as long as you want. And if you want to dance, well," she said, shaking her head, "I suppose you're grown enough."

"Aunt Esther, Papa asked Miss A'Lelia to give you and Aunt Nellie this check so that you can pay the rent up," Bessie said. "And I told Miss A'Lelia that if you didn't mind, I'd like to stay here with you until Mama and Papa come to Harlem."

"Me too," Eddie said. "I-I'd like to st-st-stay here, too."

"Oh, my Lord," Aunt Esther said, hugging them both. "You children are so sweet."

Bessie smiled and hugged her back. "After all, Aunt Esther, like Grandma used to say, 'As long as you with your family, everything is always gonna be all right.'"

A PEEK INTO THE PAST

The Janitor Who Paints
*by Harlem artist
Palmer Hayden, 1939-40*

Looking Back: 1928

In the 1920s, Harlem was one of the liveliest neighborhoods in New York City—maybe even in America. As the biggest, most prosperous African American community in the country, it drew thousands of people from all over the United States and beyond. Its rich mix of people and cultures sparked a creative explosion of African American art, music, dance, theater, and literature that became known as the *Harlem Renaissance.*

By 1915 so many African Americans lived in Harlem that it was called "the capital of Black America." During World War I, from 1915 to 1918, tens of thousands more African Americans moved there, seeking jobs and an escape from prejudice and racial violence in the South. Through the 1920s, black people looking for opportunity headed to Harlem.

Harlem was one of the few places in America where black people could be bankers, business owners, and even policemen.

Thousands of Southerners left rural homes like this and moved north for a better life.

Harlem became a melting pot, bringing together African Americans from cities, villages, and farms, from the North and the South. Immigrants came from the Caribbean—like Lillian's family and Miss Flo—and from Africa. Each group brought different dialects, foods, and musical and artistic styles. Some Harlem residents were educated, others were not. All these differences led to tensions, but the people of Harlem were united by one common experience: no matter how wealthy or educated they were, they all faced prejudice because of the color of their skin.

As Harlem grew larger, its people developed a new sense of power and unity. Political leaders like Marcus Garvey and W. E. B. Du Bois encouraged African Americans to fight for their rights and to take pride in their own traditions and experience.

One of the first big events of the Harlem Renaissance occurred in 1921, when *Shuffle Along*—an all-black musical comedy featuring exciting jazz dancing— became a smash hit on Broadway. Its success opened the way for many other black musicals and

Performers in the Broadway show **Shuffle Along**

*Duke Ellington and (below) one
of the popular jazz songs he wrote.*

dramas. For the first time, black performers achieved national stardom. Actor Paul Robeson, tap dancer Bill "Bojangles" Robinson, singers Bessie Smith and Josephine Baker, musician Louis Armstrong, and composer Duke Ellington became famous across America and Europe. Jazz dancing became an American craze. In the 1920s, *everyone* learned to dance the Charleston, just as Bessie does. Wealthy white New Yorkers flocked to Harlem's nightclubs to watch black musicians and dancers perform the hottest new music.

In spite of Harlem's popularity, prejudice against African Americans thrived. Many white nightclub owners in Harlem allowed blacks inside only if they were waiters or entertainers. In one famous incident, a black composer was barred from the nightclub where his own music was being performed.

Still, it was because of the Harlem Renaissance that jazz—which grew out

*Singer Bessie Smith became a
star in America and Europe.*

of the musical traditions of southern blacks—found national popularity. Today, jazz is enjoyed not just in the United States, but around the world.

Black writers were also part of the Harlem scene. Before the early 1900s, few books by African Americans were published. That changed during the Harlem Renaissance. Writers like W. E. B. Du Bois published powerful articles arguing for the rights of African Americans. Poets like Langston Hughes and Claude McKay gained a wide audience for their eloquent poems about black life. Jessie Redmon Fauset wrote novels about the black middle and upper classes. Zora Neale Hurston wrote stories and plays showing life among poor black farmers.

Poet Langston Hughes

Writer Zora Neale Hurston

The work of these and many other Harlem writers gave white Americans a fuller picture of black life. Readers began to see how African Americans in different parts of the country and in different economic classes really lived.

For the first time, too, black artists portrayed African American people in their work. Painters and sculptors like Aaron Douglas, Palmer Hayden, and Augusta Savage developed new artistic styles influenced by African American folk traditions, African art, and the energy of jazz. Wealthy

The painting style of Harlem artist Aaron Douglas shows the influence of African art.

art patrons sponsored contests with cash prizes for talented young artists. Carl Van Vechten, a white art critic who appears in Bessie's story, helped publicize their work. Exhibitions of work by black artists toured the country.

A'Lelia Walker—the daughter of America's first female millionaire—became a leader in the Harlem Renaissance

because of the support she gave to artists and writers. Six feet tall and a dramatic dresser, Walker was a famous figure in Harlem. In 1927, she turned her mansion into a *salon,* or social club, for artists and named it the Dark Tower, after the title of a magazine column written by Harlem poet Countee Cullen. The Dark Tower became a place where New York's leading artists, writers, musicians, and thinkers could gather and share ideas.

A'Lelia Walker, a wealthy supporter of the arts

Despite the Harlem Renaissance, black people still faced discrimination in their daily lives—in schools, housing, jobs, and even medical care. For example, whites who suffered from the deadly lung disease called *tuberculosis,* or TB, were promptly sent to government-run rest homes called *sanatoriums* for care. But blacks often ended up on sanatorium waiting lists for years. Many died while waiting.

A sanatorium for TB patients

Because TB was so feared, families of all races tried to hide the fact that a loved one had this disease. Black people who could not get into a sanatorium were often hidden away to prevent infecting others and were cared for in secret, just as Bessie's mother is.

When the Great Depression hit America in 1929, people of all races lost their savings, their jobs, and even their homes. The Depression lasted through the 1930s and ended the careers of many artists and entertainers.

Yet the Harlem Renaissance still influences America today. Harlem's writers, artists, musicians, and thinkers helped show the world the vitality and creativity of African American life. Their work enriched American culture and helped pave the way for future generations of African American artists.

Modern-day writer Toni Morrison has won the Nobel Prize and the Pulitzer Prize— the world's top awards for literature.

ABOUT THE AUTHOR

Evelyn Coleman grew up in North Carolina with her parents, her brother, Eddie Joe, and lots of relatives who lived on her street. She dreamed of being a pediatrician or a physicist, but instead she grew up to become a psychotherapist and later began a career as a writer. She says that she loves writing so much, she'd write twenty hours a day, seven days a week, if she could! Today, she lives in Atlanta, Georgia, with her husband and her dog, and enjoys spending time with her granddaughter, Taylor.

Her books for children include *White Socks Only* (Smithsonian Most Outstanding Title, 1996), *The Foot Warmer and the Crow*, *The Glass Bottle Tree*, *To Be a Drum*, and *The Riches of Osceola McCarty* (Carter G. Woodson Honor Book and Smithsonian Notable Children's Book, 1998). *White Socks Only* has been adapted as an educational film by Phoenix Films.

FREE CATALOGUE!

American Girl Gear is all about who you are today—smart, spirited, and ready for anything! Our catalogue is full of clothes and accessories that let you express yourself, with great styles for every occasion!

For your **free** catalogue, return this postcard, call **1-800-845-0005**, or visit our Web site at **www.americangirl.com**.

Send me a catalogue:

My name
_____

My address
_____

City _____ State _____ Zip 12567

My birth date: ___/___/___
　　　　　　month　day　year

Send my friend a catalogue:

My friend's name
_____

Address
_____

City _____ State _____ Zip 12575

My e-mail address
_____

Parent's signature
_____

Subscribe today to *American Girl*®– the magazine written especially for you!

For just $19.95, we'll send you 6 big bimonthly issues of **American Girl.** You'll get even more games, giggles, crafts, projects, and helpful advice. Plus, every issue is jam-packed with great stories about girls just like you!

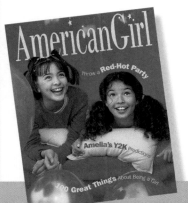

Yes! **I want to order a subscription.**
　❑ Bill me　❑ Payment enclosed

Send bill to: (please print)

Adult's name
_____

Address
_____

City _____ State _____ Zip

Send magazine to: (please print)

Girl's name
_____

Address
_____

City _____ State _____ Zip

Girl's birth date: ___/___/___
　　　　　　　month　day　year

Guarantee: You may cancel anytime for a full refund. Allow 4-6 weeks for first issue. Canadian subscription $24 U.S.　© 1999 Pleasant Company　K01L1